Treachery Trail

Also by Cliff Farrell
in Large Print:

Comanche
Desperate Journey: Western Stories

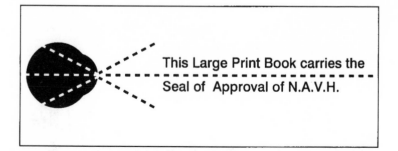

This Large Print Book carries the
Seal of Approval of N.A.V.H.

Treachery Trail

CLIFF FARRELL

Thorndike Press • Thorndike, Maine

Published in 2001 by arrangement with
Golden West Literary Agency

Thorndike Press Large Print Western Series.

The tree indicium is a trademark of Thorndike Press.

The text of this Large Print edition is unabridged.
Other aspects of the book may vary from the original edition.

Set in 16 pt. Plantin by Minnie B. Raven.

Printed in the United States on permanent paper.

Library of Congress Cataloging-in-Publication Data

Farrell, Cliff.
    Treachery trail / by Cliff Farrell.
      p. cm.
    ISBN 0-7862-3121-1 (lg. print : hc : alk. paper)
    1. Large type books. I. Title.
    PS3556.A43 T74 2001
    813′.54—dc21   00-053230

Treachery Trail

1

✳✳✳✳✳✳✳✳✳✳✳✳✳✳✳✳✳✳✳✳✳✳✳✳

The biting wind warned that autumn was over and real winter was near as Val Lang rode into Wagonbow. He held no regrets. Each passing of a season put farther from his mind the fear that Cass Irons would track him down. Like the breeze that was worrying the hoofprints of his horse in the cold, dry dust of the street, time was blotting out his past.

Arrival of winter meant that the trail-driving season was about over and he could rest easy on that score also. After eight years of it he was beginning to feel really safe, to feel almost convinced that he belonged in this adopted northern range. This thought warmed him as he racked his horse in front of Henry Erskine's Pioneer Bank. Removing the single spur he wore, he hung it on the saddle and headed for the door of the bank.

He nodded and spoke to two passing men, addressing them by their given names. They responded with quick friendliness, a trifle flattered to be on a first-name basis with the prosperous cattleman they knew by the name of Dave Land.

Dave Land! Val was becoming so accustomed to his assumed name he often had the chill feeling he was forgetting his real identity. He kept remembering the good days when he had been a young, wild, irresponsible cowboy, a top hand on the *Si-Si* down on the Pecos. Sometimes at night he came violently awake from dreams that he had again been riding with the old crew — Red Mike Murphy, Shorty, Miguel. Above all, with Boone Irons. Boone, who was in his grave and for whose murder Cass Irons had vowed at his son's funeral to personally hang Val Lang.

Still, it hardly seemed reasonable that the determination of even a man like Cass Irons could bridge the gap of eight years. It was over. This was Wagonbow in Wyoming Territory on the Deadwood trail and Cass C. Irons was down on his big *Si-Si* ranch west of the Pecos in New Mexico.

Val's bootheels thudded on the plank floor of the bank as he entered and shouldered the door shut against the thrust of the wind. It was unpleasantly warm in the place. Henry, as usual, had the pot belly of the big cannon stove glowing red. Henry even wore woolen underwear during the blazing heat of summer.

Henry was at the cashier's window, haggling with a depositor over some financial matter. He waved his hand to Val and tripped the foot lever that freed the door into the cage. He motioned toward the entrance to his private office, a privilege only for those whose presence meant a potential profit, a category that included a prospective son-in-law like Val.

He slid out of his heavy saddle coat, entered the small office and took a chair, hoisting a boot onto the corner of the table that served as Henry's desk which was scarred by much similar use. It was a bench-made boot that had seen considerable service also, but had the comfortable look of ease and the patina that told of care and pride of appearance.

That same good quality extended to his garb. He wore a dark gray, double-breasted woolen shirt and dark, pin-striped saddle trousers that were of best tailoring and kept carefully pressed by the Indian wife of his half-breed cowhand. He stood taller than average. While he had never been called on to prove it as far as anyone in Wagonbow knew, he looked like he could very well take care of himself in case of trouble. He had always stayed clear of serious disputes.

A rifle was slung in the boot of his saddle but he had never been known to carry a sidearm in town where the majority of the males did not consider themselves fully clothed without at least one six-shooter as part of their array.

He had a good forehead and crisp dark hair. A jarring note was the very thick, very black beard that hid the line of his jaws and chin so that it was impossible to determine their exact cut. He had gray eyes beneath thick dark brows. Men took it for granted that his age was in the forties. That was mainly due to the beard, but also because he had built up a record as a very experienced dealer in livestock and land who was on his way to becoming well-to-do.

This last opinion was true, but estimates of his age were well off the mark. He had actually not yet reached his thirtieth birthday. The beard helped conceal many things.

He rolled a cigarette, tilted his chair back and waited. Dusty red velvet curtains covered the lower half of the window at his elbow, giving privacy from passersby on the sidewalk who were arm's reach from the glass. The curtain was not entirely closed, giving him a slit through which he could see. Army Street, which led to Fort Miles, half a mile west of town, was Wagonbow's heart.

Through the peephole Val could see the small silhouette of a sentry's head and shoulders above the fort's stockade. Two score of Indian lodges were scattered around the fort and along the bluff above Beaver River. Smoke drifted from the wind wings, squaws and children moved about the camp. These were the lodges of the Crows who wore army uniforms and scouted for the cavalry in the endless campaign against their traditional enemies, the Sioux and the Cheyenne.

The town was only drowsily active. The wives of three officers passed by in an army wagon, drawn by mules, with an escort of two armed orderlies. They had filled market baskets after a session at Wagonbow's stores. The shabby wagon of a homesteader stood before a blacksmith shop. Two Crow children and three town urchins squabbled over a marble game on a lot across the street.

Half a dozen cowponies were racked at Pat McMullen's Golden Elk saloon across the way. Val gave the brands of the horses careful scrutiny. He relaxed. They were from a Texas outfit that had failed to find a market this late in season at Ogalalla and Julesburg and were laying over while the owners scouted for range that would carry the cattle over spring.

They had arrived at Wagonbow more than a week ago and Val had sized them up previously. They were from around the Brazos River in Texas and he was sure all members of the crew were strangers to him. The Brazos was a long way from where Cass Irons ran his *Si-Si* cattle in New Mexico. Val had never been in the Brazos country and it wasn't likely that any of the Texas riders who were in the saloon had ever wandered into New Mexico — at least into *Si-Si* territory. Still it was best not to take chances, and he intended to keep out of their sight, just as he had avoided personal contact with all the men of the cattle drives that had come through during his years here in the Territory.

It had been a growing problem with him the past two or three years. Despite the fierce hostility of the Sioux, cattlemen were moving into northern range, planting their spurs deep and hanging on. The power of the tribes was waning although war parties still ranged the wild country north of Wagonbow. They ambushed small wagon trains, but the trail bosses hired a score or more of armed men at Julesburg or Cheyenne to flank their drives and usually went through unchallenged.

The bulk of the cattle that were being moved north came from the overgrazed ranches of Texas where owners were weary of fighting ticks, drought and the inroads of barbed wire. However, now and then herds bearing brands from New Mexico had passed through the Wagonbow country. At such times Val had seen to it that he had business far away, in Kansas City or Omaha.

Even now, although the odds were heavily in his favor, he felt the old chill, the old help-lessness, when he read a brand from southern range. It angered him to realize that right now, after eight years of it, his fingers grew tense, his stomach tightened at the mere thought of it.

The cow punchers came shouldering out of the Golden Elk, laughing and carefree. They mounted and headed out of town, their mounts lifting a clatter of hoofs. They were on their way back to their wagon camp and the cattle herd.

Val again made sure he had never laid eyes on any of them before. The tension faded. He blew smoke toward the ceiling. Men and women passed by on the sidewalk. Some wore the homespun and calico of home-steaders. Their numbers were growing few. They had come in when the army had established Fort Miles as the strongpoint for jumping off for the Dakota mines on the Deadwood Trail. They had learned that the land was not free at all. They had to earn it, fight for it against the Sioux who still claimed ownership, but, above all, against nature itself.

These were people from gentler lands, from Missouri, Illinois, Kentucky, Ohio. Places where trees grew, pastures remained green all summer, where rain fell in plenty. Here on the plains their corn patches were eaten by jackrabbits or grasshoppers, or withered in the blazing sun of July. The country was too dry for the garden vegetables they had depended on to feed their children and themselves. Prairie dogs ate the roots of their fruit trees.

Some of them had frozen in their sod houses or dug-outs during the bitter winters. Some had been scalped. These latter were the bold ones who had dared settle north of Red Buttes. All that remained of their efforts were ruined abodes and graves.

Val fingered his beard. He detested the adornment, but was chained to it. Eight years was not long enough to make Cass Irons forget. Not even a lifetime. However, surely, time would eventually change him so that even the grim ranchman would never recognize him. Then he could shave off the beard and feel younger again.

Henry Erskine finished his negotiations at the window and came into the office, settling himself in the swivel chair at the table. "Afternoon, David," he said. "Jenny Jane will be along directly. She'll fetch the buggy down from the house to drive me home."

"I'm expecting her," Val said. "I sent word by Benny Feather to arrive early. I might want to borrow your rig for an hour or so, Henry."

"Welcome, David," Henry boomed. "Always welcome to anything I have."

The name he had adopted, David Land, was a good quiet term that fitted a man who was pushing ahead by hard work and by understanding this land, its limitations and its possibilities.

"I want to show Jane the house," he said. "It's about ready. They hung the parlor door yesterday and cleaned out their tools and such. The door is real pretty. Stained glass in all colors. I hope Jane likes it."

"I'll be mighty proud to have you in the family, David," Henry said. "You're a comer. A go-gitter. Jenny Jane's a lucky gal to have a chance like that. But she deserves it."

Val winced inwardly. A chance? Henry, as

usual, was putting it on a dollars and cents basis. He also cringed at the double-handed term her father always used. Jenny Jane was his pet name for her, but, to Val, it did not fit the handsome, practical-minded young lady he had made up his mind to ask to marry him.

"It isn't settled yet," he reminded Henry. "Jane's the one to decide it."

Henry smiled complacently. "But I warn you not to put it off too long," he chuckled. "There are a lot o' other young sprouts around here that would jump if'n she cracked the whip. You know how gals are. Jenny Jane ain't the kind to wait around."

Val changed the subject. "I've also got another matter in mind," he said. "I've made Ed Blake an offer for his claim up on the Antelope Fork. He's got a patent on it. He wants to pull out of the country."

Henry instantly became a shrewd banker. "What do you want his place fer?"

"I need a little more grazing room. Ed's homestead fronts on the Antelope. There's always water in that stretch in dry years and there's buffalo grass where he hasn't cleared for crops. I've got about forty head of new stock that needs doctoring and fattening through the winter. Ed's place will help out. In addition that land will give me legal

16

rights across the Antelope into government open range as far as the bluffs."

"You're buyin' up crips from that Texas outfit thet's layin' over on Sage Crick, ain't you?" Henry said, aggrieved. "I heerd thet wolves stampeded 'em a few nights ago an' they lost a lot of steers in them coulees."

He leaned forward, "How much did Charlie pay fer 'em, David? How high did you authorize him to go?"

"Six a head," Val said, smiling at the horror in Henry's expression.

"Six a head!" Henry moaned. "That's just plain, downright stealin', David. They was worth more'n that. Why, I'd have give seven a head myself. Maybe eight."

"Some are in bad shape," Val said. "I'll lose some of them. I had to take everything that was on its feet, no weeding out or picking. Charlie Summers is doctoring the bunch, but he can't pull them all through. I'll have to carry the others through the winter to get them up to market value. That's where Ed's buffalo grass will help out. It's near enough to my place that I can handle them along with what other stuff I have."

"You still stand to make a pretty penny," Henry snorted. "A thousand percent on your money, maybe. I suppose you want a

17

loan to swing the deal for Ed's place?"

Val nodded. "I'm a little short of ready cash at the moment. I've got every dollar working. I've got money coming from that beef I sold at K.C., but it won't come through until after the first of the month. I paid for the cripples in cash."

"You mean you gave the money to Charlie Summers to pay for 'em," Henry said caustically. "I still don't see why you bother havin' Charlie do your stock-buyin'."

Henry did not know it, but he was venturing into dangerous ground. "I've told you before that Charlie's a whiz at judging stock and driving a bargain," Val explained.

"You drive a hard enough bargain when we do business," Henry complained. "Seems to me like a waste o' money, workin' through a professional stock trader like Charlie. How much commission do you pay him?"

"Just enough to keep us both happy," Val said.

"Bah!" Henry sniffed. Val's success at buying up drag and crippled cattle from passing trail drives at bargain prices and turning them into marketable beef was a sore point with Henry who felt that he was the one who should be reaping the profits. He had tried to compete with Val in the

18

business in the past, but had found that bringing lame and ailing stock into prime shape required a certain talent and hard work — also the proper sheltered range and grazing. Val possessed all these necessities. Henry did not have the time nor the ability, and the men he hired had turned out to be incompetent.

Val turned over the actual bargaining for the hospital stock to Charlie Summers, the portly owner of Wagonbow's principal livery and freighting yard. Charlie was a famed horse and cattle trader who was said to have never been bested in a deal. His skill was Val's ostensible reason for having him act as agent in dickering with herd owners or trail bosses. Nobody, not even Charlie, knew the truth was that Val did not want to meet a southern cowman face-to-face if it could be avoided.

"How much you offerin' Ed Blake fer his place?" Henry demanded.

"Six-fifty," Val said.

Henry's scraggy brows fluttered disbelievingly. He was a small pouter-pigeon of a man, round-stomached, bandy-legged with a yellowish bald pate surrounded by a fringe of dusty, clay-colored hair. A heavy gold watchchain was always draped across his stomach from the pockets of his black

19

vest. He suffered from bunions and wore broken-down carpet slippers when he was in the bank.

"Six-fifty!" he echoed. "Six hundred an' fifty *dollars?* You don't mean that, David."

"Why not?"

"This man is runnin' scared, son. So's his wife. They know some o' Crazy Horse's braves has hit everything north o' the buttes an' everybody expects 'em to hit south, too, like they used to. Besides, Ed Blake's found out he can't make a go of it, farmin'. All he wants is to git out o' the country with whole skin an' a few dollars. He'd sell for a lot less."

"His place is worth it."

"Offer him three-fifty, an' he'd jump at it. Maybe three hundred even."

"They've got three young ones," Val said. "Ed's got to get his family back to Illinois. That'll take money. Then they'll need something to live on until he gets on his feet back there."

Henry was angry. "That ain't none o' your worry. An' it ain't any way to do business. You'll be spoilin' folks. I've been pickin' up land patents fer a song. There are others about ready to light out. When they hear about this they'll expect big prices too."

"I need Ed's place," Val said. "Need it

right now. If I can build up that crippled stock before real winter comes, I might make enough to pay for his place and a little over."

Henry's eyes became crafty. "What if I offered Ed Blake seven hundred?" he asked. "Then where'd you be? Stuck with them crippled cows. I could hold you up fer a bigger price, now couldn't I?"

Val laughed. He turned to the window, parted the curtains and pointed. The shabby wagon still stood in front of the blacksmith shop. In it now sat a man and wife with three small children crowded around them. "Try it," he said. "There's Ed and his family. He's waiting to hear if I got the loan from you. I told him to be in town about this time today."

Henry pursed his lips, wishing he hadn't got himself into such an awkward position. "I was just givin' you a lesson in business, David," he said hastily. "O' course, I wouldn't bid agin you, bein' as you're goin' to be in the family."

"Ed shook hands with me on it," Val said. "He's a man who stands by his word. So do I. There are lots of people in this world like that."

"All right, all right!" Henry said. "I'll draw up the papers. Eight percent. Now, come to think it, rates are goin' up. I'll have to charge eight an' a half."

"A sixty-day note," Val said. "Six percent."

"Now, David, that's imposin' on a friendship. As head o' this bank I can't —"

Val chuckled. "Bill Oates, down at the hotel, can handle it for me at six percent. He told me only a few days ago he had some money that he'd like to put out. Fact is, he said something about five and a half percent. I figure I could get it from him for five if I dickered."

Henry sighed. "You're a hard man to bargain with, David. I'll fix up the note. Just how the bank's goin' to git along, puttin' out money at six percent, I don't know. I've got big expenses to meet."

Val watched, amused, as Henry pulled a pad of forms from a drawer and began filling out the terms of a promissory note, his pen rasping. He was accustomed to Henry's parsimony. It was commonly said Henry still had the first dollar in interest the bank had earned cached away in its vault.

"Give the money to Ed," he said. He parted the curtains wider and waved to the watching homesteader, who at once alighted from the wagon and headed for the bank.

He looked at the clock on the wall. "Jane

ought to be showing up," he said. "I want to get her back here before dark."

His voice trailed off. Two heavily laden prairie wagons with canvas hoods came rolling past the bank. Mud still dripped from spokes and felloes, and from the bellies and legs of the six-mule teams that were in harness, showing that they had just forded the Beaver below town.

Covered wagons were as common as the time of day in Wagonbow which was a supply point for the army as well as the jumping off place for freighters and travelers heading up the Deadwood Trail to the Dakota mountains.

These vehicles had come a long, hard distance. They were big, scow-bodied, with long reaches and made so they could be raised on their bolsters for fording deep streams. They were not eastern-built. There was something Spanish in the cut of their bodies and the tilt of the bows. These had been made in Texas or perhaps El Paso. Maybe even by the wagon builders of Chihuahua. It was wagons of this type Val had known all his life before he fled from New Mexico.

Two Negro drivers rode the off wheelers. Each had big old-style cap and ball Dragoon pistols in holsters that were slung on the collars of their mounts. Repeating Winchesters were scabbarded within reach on the wagons. The vehicles were fitted with loopholes in their plank sides. One of the wagons was apparently used as sleeping quarters, for Val glimpsed hats and feminine garments hanging inside.

Eight men flanked the wagons. Two were Mexicans, but sun and weather had burned the skin of the others equally dark. The Mexicans were dressed in the style of *vaqueros* and some of the others had on items that came from the same love of color. All apparel had the marks of wear and tear, showing their owners had traveled the same hard trail as the wagons. Each of the eight men was armed with at least one pistol, bowie knives and rifles. There could be no mistaking their origin. These were riders from west of the Pecos where Mexico still swayed the customs and dress.

Above all, he had recognized the big-jawed, wide-shouldered man who rode in the lead on the left flank, mounted on a powerful black horse. A new clatter of hoofs arose and he chanced another glimpse. A Mexican wrangler was hazing the remuda of a score of horses and mules down the street in the wake of the wagons.

Val dropped the curtain and tried to make

himself smaller in his chair. None of the passing riders had glanced in the direction of the bank but he had seen the brands on the mules and saddlestock. He had recognized at least three of the cowboys.

He again withdrew from the window. The chill that was always latent within him came to icy life. Now, after eight years, when he had started to believe it was really over, it had happened, the thing he had feared. Some of those cowhands who had rode past were strangers to him. In eight years many of the crew would have drifted away and new ones been hired.

But the faces he remembered would also remember his face. The Mexican wrangler was Miguel Ortes with whom he had traded banter and shared tobacco many times when he had been a top hand with the *Si-Si*, Cass Irons' outfit down in the Pecos country. The chunky, flame-haired, grinning cowboy who had winked at a girl as he rode past was Red Mike Murphy, the wild Irishman who had a grin that could melt butter and a temper as explosive as a firecracker. And Shorty Long, the harmonica whiz.

Worse yet, the big man who rode a fine, powerful black horse, was Zack Roper himself. Zack, range boss of the *Si-Si*, along with Cass Irons, had sworn to personally yank on the rope that would hang Valentine Lang for the murder of Boone Irons.

Val knew all these men well. They had been saddle partners, friends when he had ridden for the C-Bar-C. He still kept instinctively trying to make himself smaller in the chair, straining his ears, expecting them to stop and come into the bank. Surely there could be only one reason why the crew from the *Si-Si* would be here in Wyoming Territory on this cold afternoon.

But the wagons continued creaking down the street with the remuda following. He heard the Negro drivers grunt orders and the vehicles halted, evidently at John Wisk's mercantile a distance from the bank. A distance, but, to Val, not a safe distance.

He found that Henry was eying him questioningly. "Anything wrong?" Henry asked.

"Wrong? No. Why?" He felt he had made the denial too swiftly, too vigorously.

Henry must have thought so also, for he studied him a moment longer before passing over the promissory note to be signed. He was aware he was still being surveyed speculatively by the banker as he scratched his name on the paper.

"Do you know them fellers that just went by?" Henry asked.

"Who are they?" Val asked.

"I don't know any of 'em by name, but they're ridin' stock that belongs to a cattleman named Cass C. Irons. You've heard of *him*, I reckon."

"Can't say I have," Val said, striving to appear casual. "Now, wait a minute. Seems to me I have at that. Isn't he from somewhere down south? Texas?"

"New Mexico," Henry said. "Pretty well known down that way and elsewhere. He was a pioneer. Fightin' man. Cleaned out the Apaches, then the rustlers an' outlaws. Served a few terms in the Territorial Legislature. Turned down a chance to be gov'nor. Built up a big ranch. Main brand is what you saw on them mules an' hawses. C-Bar-C. They call it the *Si-Si* down there. Like they say it in Mexico. Yes. Yes."

"This Cass C. Irons couldn't have been one of that bunch," Val remarked. "From all you say about him he must be up in years."

"He ain't so old, at that. Past fifty, I reckon. But he wasn't one of 'em. He come through here last summer, along in July, it was with two drives of stock cattle, headin' for the Dakota country to set up a new ranch. I got acquainted with him while he was in Wagonbow."

"Is he branching out into northern range

27

like some of them from down there?" Val asked.

"Nope. He's movin' the *Si-Si*, lock, stock an' whisky barrel on up to Dakota Territory. Figures he could git rich faster, I reckon. Said that Pecos country is too damned dry to raise anything but longhorns and mavericks. He aims to go into these here white-faced breeds that grow better beef. He had up to six thousand head of cows and young stuff in two herds. Town was full of *Si-Si* riders for nigh onto a week. He'd hired a lot of tough men who knew how to shoot to ride through the Sioux country with the herds. They'd like to have bought out the stores, outfittin' for the trip. An' they sure did buy out all the likker."

"That must have been while I was in Omaha, marketing that jag of beef," Val said.

"Come to think of it, you're right," Henry said.

Val felt a little limp at the thought of his narrow escape. He had really gone east to avoid the men of a trail drive that had originated in the hill country of south Texas, although he also had legitimate business matters to care for in Omaha. Luck had kept him out of the way of Cass Irons. Cass had been right here in Wagonbow during his absence. Cass Irons, who had eyes the color of steel and were about as hard. They looked right through a man and never forgot what they saw. Eight years in time and the beard might not have fooled him.

"Them wagons out there are carryin' household furniture an' the rest of the Irons family from the looks," Henry was saying. "Cass Irons mentioned thet he had a daughter an' a young granddaughter who'd be along before snow flew. Looks like them's the two gittin' off the wagons."

Henry had parted the curtains wide and was gazing down the street. Val hesitated, then peered over Henry's shoulder. The two big wagons had halted in front of the mercantile. The drivers were freeing the teams from the vehicles, preparatory to heading them toward Charlie Summers' livery where they evidently would be treated with rations of grain.

Zack Roper and his crew had tied up their horses in front of the Golden Elk and were jingling their spurs into the saloon, wiping their lips in anticipation.

A slim young woman and a girl of about eight had alighted from the wagons and stood on the sidewalk. They wore bonnets and heavy winter garb. Val knew he was looking at the sister of the man for whose murder he was wanted. Cass Irons had put up $10,000 in gold at a Santa Fe bank, payable to any man who brought in Val dead or alive.

The child must surely be the niece of Boone Irons whose body lay in an expensive marble memorial on the *Si-Si* ranch, along with that of his older brother, Wyatt. Sheila Irons, who stood smiling down at little Penny Irons, was the last of Cass Irons' three children.

2

****

Val knew what he was risking as he continued to gaze. Sheila Irons stood for a time brushing dust from her skirt and that of the child. She adjusted Penny's bonnet and her own. They were laughing gaily. Penny walked duck-legged for a few steps, exaggerating the effect of being on solid ground after miles that day in the roughness of the wagon.

Sheila opened her reticule, spoke to the drivers and handed them coins and wagged a finger at them in a mock warning. The two men, grinning, headed for the rear door of the Golden Elk, for they were not privileged to enter the establishment and must drink their beer among the ash heaps at the rear.

Val's eyes followed Sheila Irons as she and her niece entered the mercantile. If any of the arrivals were to recognize him on sight, he felt she would likely be the one. The eyes of a sister might even be more discerning than that of a father.

Cass Irons had loved his two sons, but all

three of them had worshiped Sheila and had been putty in her hands. Cass Irons had made what amounted to a holy crusade in trying to find Val and avenge the death of Boone. He had hired the Pinkertons to ransack the West. He had seen to it that the reward posters were tacked up in every post office, every railroad and stagecoach station, every law office from border to border.

Luck had a big hand in the fact that Val was still alive and free. Luck along with the wits and endurance that had made him Cass Irons' top hand with the *Si-Si* and that meant that he had cow savvy in addition to being able to ride and rope with the best of them for Cass hired only men who knew their business.

For more than a year he had blinded his trails, backtracked, hidden in big Midwest cities and in the wild thickets along the Texas border where he had camped with other wanted men and had learned from them more of the art of dodging capture. He had survived narrow escapes at being trapped by the Pinkertons who were shrewd and relentless. He had finally reached Wagonbow, and after months of remaining alert had decided he had at last thrown them off.

He had been right as far as the Pinkertons were concerned. But now, after eight years, Sheila Irons was here as well as Zack Roper. Sheila had changed, of course. She had been a colt-legged, imperious spitfire who spent her winters away from the ranch at school in Santa Fe and who forgot all that training when she returned to the *Sí-Sí* in the summers. She could use a rifle as well as the average man on a hunt for game and could heel calves expertly with a drag loop when an extra hand was needed at the branding fires.

Now she was a young woman of about twenty-two, heading for new country to help her father pioneer virgin range, just as Cass Irons and his bride had pioneered the Pecos country in the days when the Comanches and Apaches were riding.

Val became aware Henry Erskine was eying him with growing curiosity. He settled back in his chair once more and stabbed out the nub of his cigarette in an ashtray. He could not help glancing down the street once more through the window. Sheila and the child had vanished into John Wisk's general store.

"Here comes Jenny Jane," Henry said. "Ain't she purty?"

Jane Erskine drove past the bank in

Henry's gleaming top buggy with its plump bay mare in harness, wheeled off the street into the hitch lot at the rear. Val arose and met her at the door as she entered after tethering the mare in the lot.

He pulled out his watch, frowning at her. She smiled and twitted his nose with her forefinger. "No sermons, my tall and frowning friend," she said. "After all I'm not very late. I had trouble with my hair, with my dress, with everything. I'm in no mood to be called on the carpet."

She always had a talent for appearing as though she had just stepped out of a bandbox. A scrubbed-hygienic look, with every stitch and strand exactly in place. A composed, dark-haired, dark-eyed young lady, she was especially well turned-out at the moment in a powder gray dress and fur-trimmed jacket with puffed sleeves. A tiny hat was perched on her hair. She had no patience with disorder in others. Or tardiness, although she did not extend that rule to herself.

He moved to kiss her, but she smilingly pushed him back. "That isn't proper, David," she said. "Worse yet, you'll undo all my efforts at being presentable."

He knew she was aware this was to be a special occasion. There was high excitement in her, throbbing anticipation. He touched her cheek with the points of his fingers, his throat suddenly tight with the knowledge that all this happiness might end for both of them soon. In fairness to her he must tell her what had taken place in the past. It was a problem that had burdened his conscience for months, ever since he had known that she expected him to ask her to marry him. She was sure this was the day he would ask her to become his wife, and she was right.

"I've got something to show you," he said. "I'm borrowing your father's rig for an hour or two."

He added, "It's a secret — I hope."

Mischief danced in her eyes. He was certain it was actually no secret with her, but she was keeping up the pretense. For the past three months masons and carpenters and glaziers had been building a new house not far from the old sod-built man's place he occupied on his holdings three miles out of town, on the Deadwood Trail. It had never been mentioned between them, but in a community as small as Wagonbow such things were common news.

She pretended dismay, gazing down at her dress. "It's lucky I put my duster in the buggy," she said. "The dust's ankle-deep on the trail from the looks. What are we going to look at this time, David? More buffalo grass that you want to buy? More lame cattle in smelly pens?"

He laughed, taking her arm and headed her toward the door. Her father shouted after them, "Be danged sure you two are back by six o'clock. I don't hanker to walk clean home the way my bunions are actin' up."

"You can catch a ride with most anyone, you old fraud," Jane called back.

Val was thankful she had left the rig back of the bank rather than on the street. The *Si-Si* wagons still stood deserted in front of the mercantile. Roper and the *Si-Si* crew were still in the Golden Elk. Val paused long enough to draw the rifle from the boot of the saddle on his horse at the rail, then he and Jane turned the corner and walked to the buggy at the rear. He drew a deeper breath.

He helped her into the seat, untethered the horse and took over the reins, heading the mare down the town's side street, turning into a backstreet that was given over to freight sheds, railroad sidings and shacks.

"I declare, David," Jane protested. "This is hardly my idea of the best way out of town. I feel as though I need another bath already. Are you ashamed to display me on Army Street?"

"Now that's exactly it," he said. "I'd have to be using the whip on some of those fellows to keep them away from you."

She laid a hand on his arm. "You're very mean for not telling me what you have for a surprise. What is it? Where is it?"

"Keep guessing," he said.

The road joined with the main northward trail at the fringe of the settlement. This trail wound through the Sioux hunting grounds, terminating three hundred miles north in the Dakota mining camps.

Each turn of the wheels put distance between him and Sheila Irons and Zack Roper. The *Si-Si* people might stay at Wagonbow overnight, but it was likely they would be advised to move on to the Sage Creek ford an hour's drive up the trail where there was timber for firewood, a shallow, clear stream and ample grazing for the stock.

"It's been a good year for cattle," Val said. "The buffalo grass and grama have come through the best I've seen. No cow or horse with the ambition to rustle should starve this winter even on open range."

"Is that what you brought me out here to talk about?" Jane sniffed.

He drew her near and tried to kiss her. "You're like a bear, David," she protested. "If you ruffled my feathers, people would see it when we got back to town and they'd imagine all kinds of things."

"I doubt if talk would ruffle your feathers, darling," he said. "You are not the kind to let other people run your life."

She laughed. "Is that supposed to be flattering? I'm afraid that you see through my surface." After a moment, she added, "But I wonder if I have ever seen through yours, David."

He looked swiftly at her. "Now that's an odd thing to say. I thought I was an open book."

"Whenever I opened that book I've found nothing to read that I fully understand," she said slowly. "I wonder what you're like beneath that beard. What you're really like. That awful beard. I want you to get rid of it."

"You're hitting me where it hurts," he protested. "My vanity. I'd be lost without my beard. It gives me dignity. Other men respect me more. Maybe you've noticed that important men wear beards."

"You're evading the point. Others might wear beards to make them *appear* important. It only detracts from you. It does you no good. You are a handsome man."

"We were talking about buffalo grass. It means more than beards to both of us. I'm buying the Blake homestead which lies off to the northeast on the Antelope. My holdings will stretch all the way to open range. I can soon begin to expand, build up a brand in my own right. With a little luck and common sense I could own two, three thousand head in less than five years."

"If the Indians don't run them off," she said. "Or scalp you in the bargain."

"There's been no Indian trouble south of Red Buttes for a long time," he said. "The army is getting them in hand. The Indian war is about over."

"I doubt if General Custer would believe that," she said. "Nor a lot of others who've been killed up there."

She was shuddering. As a young girl she had nearly lost her life while visiting relatives at Julesburg when the town had been raided and burned by nearly a thousand Sioux and Cheyennes. Along with others she had raced on foot to Fort Sedgwick nearly two miles away with warriors in pursuit. She had a purple scar from an arrow graze on her forearm as a relic.

"The Sioux are still riding," Val acknowledged. "At least the young braves, but the

Custer affair has finally jolted the army into action. In another year the Sioux will all be on reservation."

Wagonbow's rooftops sank below the swells behind them. The dugouts or sod houses of homesteaders dotted the rolling plain here and there. Some were already deserted but chimney smoke from others rose into the wintry sky. The flag on the tall staff at the fort offered a glint of color off toward the Beaver.

"A person would think they'd have more getup to them," Jane spoke.

"Getup? Who?"

"These farmers, living in soddies, picking buffalo bones, wearing patches and tatters. Above all I don't see how they can stand the loneliness."

"I picked a few buffalo bones myself the first year or two," Val said. "It earned me eating money. I'd do it again if I had to."

"You're different. You've got a head on your shoulders, David. They'll still be huddling in soddies or living on charity when you're rich and living in a mansion in a city."

"Some of them, maybe. But others will make a go of it and live in mansions too. The tough ones."

He quit talking. The trail had carried them into sight of the new house. It stood on the south slope of a long swell where the winter sun would be warmer and be protected from the drive of north winds. It was a tall house, two stories to the eaves with high gables that enclosed ample attic space. Dormers pushed through the attic roof. A veranda stood along the front and sides. A bay window added space to what evidently was the parlor. A fine French-type door with tinted glass in all shades of the rainbow opened off the veranda.

A distance south of the new house squatted the sod and rock structure where Val lived. Originally it had been a small, half-dugout, but additions had been added. It now accommodated Benny Feather and his Shoshone wife who were Val's hired hands. Corrals and shed flanked the sod structure.

Val halted the buggy and waited. Jane stood up, gazing at the new house.

"I like it, David," she finally said. "It is very nice. However, I wish you had seen to it that another dormer was built into that big attic. It needs light and coolness, and circulation of air in summer. Another window would have been a help in the kitchen for the same reason. That bay window in the parlor will need large awnings in summer, being on the west instead of the east, to shut

41

out the sun. And . . ."

Her voice trailed off as she saw the growing hurt in his expression.

"Oh, I'm sorry, David," she said hastily. "I must confess I've been here before. When you weren't around. I knew you wanted it to be a secret. It really doesn't matter. After all you really didn't expect me to stay away, did you? Please don't look like I've done something awful. Don't be so childish."

She leaned her head against his shoulder. "After all, I had more than a passing interest in this house, you know."

"Of course," he said, and tried to put the disappointment out of his mind.

He drove the buggy to the veranda steps, alighted and helped her down. "See how tall it is," he said, pointing to the gable tip with pride. "It's the tallest house in these parts. I didn't see any higher ones in Omaha."

"It is very nice," she said. She looked around. "It would also be nice if there were neighbors closer."

"Neighbors? All the land you see will belong to us. But there'll be Benny Feather and Mary. They'll take over all of the sod house after we — I — get settled in the new place. In a year or so I'll be putting on riders as the herd builds up. There'll be plenty of people around."

She wrinkled her nose at him. "You are a shy man, David. You and I know that this is to be our house. Why not say it right out? Everyone takes it for granted we are going to be married." She was silent a moment, then added, "But . . ."

She stood waiting. He finished it for her. "But I've never asked you."

He walked her up the steps of the unpainted veranda. He had a key in his pocket and unlocked the fine door with the colored glass. He lifted her off her feet and carried her across the threshold. "I promised myself I'd do that the first time you came into this house with me," he told her as he sat her back on her feet.

She straightened her bonnet. "Exactly what is it you have to tell me, David?" she asked.

He gazed at her, taken aback. "Why do you say that?"

"You didn't bring me out here just to show me the house. You really must have been aware I knew about it and had already been here. You have something else to tell me."

"I thought I'd kept it hidden," he said.

"It's been on your mind for weeks. Months. Ever since you first became interested in me. It has stood between us. That's the truth, isn't it, David?"

"Yes."

"It's the reason you've put off asking me to marry you, isn't it?"

He moved into the parlor and to the bay window — the window she felt was in the wrong place. It commanded a view of the range that he liked to gaze at, especially at this waning time of day with its changing patterns, its shift of colors. The house stood high enough so that the shake roofs of the two-story officers' quarters at the fort were visible, along with the flagstaff. Wagonbow itself was hidden by the rise of the land to the southeast, but the smoke from its chimneys stained the sky in that direction. Red Buttes, twenty miles to the north, stretched across the land for miles, forming a Chinese wall beyond which glinted the higher ridges of rough country. A dozen horses grazed in a fenced pasture. A windmill creaked, supplying the watering tank. His sod house looked back at him from its eye-like windows on the flat below. His soddie, his horses, his land. To him none of this could ever be lonely. This was where he had planned to live his life. And those plans all revolved around Jane Erskine.

He turned, facing her. "My name is not David Land," he said. "My name is really

44

Valentine Lang. More than eight years ago Boone Irons, the son of a cattleman named Cass C. Irons, was murdered as he rode along a trail down in New Mexico. Boone Irons and I had a quarrel and traded a few punches with our fists in a *cantina* in town that night. They found evidence that I was the man who had shot him in the back as he rode home afterward. Cass Irons and his crew were out to lynch me, but I got away."

Jane's eyes were wide with horror. All color had gone from her face. "I — I never dreamed it would be anything like that," she stammered.

She added imploringly, "You didn't do it, did you?"

"I couldn't have done it," he said.

"What do you mean you *couldn't* have done it? Don't you know?"

"Boone and I were friends. That wasn't the first time we'd taken punches at each other. We were a couple of hotheads. We were too much alike. Always trying to beat the other at anything from roping a bear to trying to take each other's girls away. Young hellions. My father had been foreman of the Irons ranch for years. I grew up on the ranch. He died when I was fourteen. My mother had died several years before that."

"Why are you wanted for this murder?"

45

"Boone and me started out by trying to show that we could hold our liquor better than the other. It was Saturday night and had been payday at the ranch. Everybody was living it high. Neither of us had any experience at drinking. In fact I doubt if Boone had had more than half a dozen drinks in his life. I know I hadn't. All I know is that it hit me hard. Boone and me got into some kind of an argument. We always did. He took a punch at me, I took a swing at him. That's about the last I remember."

Her voice was hardly audible as she asked, "You — you don't mean you can't remember what happened? That you might have actually killed him."

"I can't believe it," he said exhaustedly. "I've lived with this thing every minute, every second ever since. Especially at night I live with it. I couldn't have done it. Boone was like a brother to me. The only brother I ever had."

"But why do they say you did it?"

"He was shot in the back with a bullet like the ones I used in my pistol. I carried around one of those old-style .36 cap-and-ball Colts in those days. It was a show-off thing, of course, something to be different. Everybody was carrying cartridge guns by that time, of course. I moulded my own bullets. It was a heavy piece of artillery, but I liked to swagger around with it on my hip."

He added, "I was young and a little fritter-brained in those days. Anyway, Boone was shot on the trail somewhere before daybreak. He didn't leave town until after midnight. That was a couple hours after we'd had our fight. Everybody said the fight didn't amount to anything, but Cass Irons' foreman, who was present and who parted us, said I told him I'd kill Boone."

"But surely there must have been more guns of that kind that someone else could have used."

"It wasn't only the gun. I was wearing corduroy saddle pants, the kind with the ridges in. That was just to be different, too. Most everybody else wore denims or hardtwist. They found the knee-mark of corduroy where someone had hunkered down in wet sand at the margin of a creek ford in the brush to get a bead on Boone against the stars as he rode by."

He waited for her to speak. He wanted her to speak, wanted understanding. But she only stood there.

"All I remember," he went on slowly, "is Zack Roper leading me to my horse and telling me to go to the ranch and sleep it off. I woke up at daybreak in the hayloft of the

47

barn at *Sí-Sí*. I hadn't been able to make it to the bunkhouse. What woke me up was a commotion in the ranch yard. They were looking for me."

"Who?"

"Cass Irons and the crew. Cass was acting like a madman. He kept screaming for me to come out and face him. He said he'd spread-eagle me between teams of work oxen and quarter me. It was the second son he'd lost. Boone's older brother, Wyatt, had been killed a couple of months earlier when the cinches broke as he busted a steer on a downslant in the hills. Cass and his sons had been mighty close."

"What did you do?"

"I didn't know at that moment why Cass had gone loco, but I knew I'd be killed if I went out there. I slipped out of the loft by the far end, got away into the brush and hid out. I heard them telling about Boone being murdered and then I knew why they were after me. I still had my old .36 Colt, but one chamber had been fired. I got to the crick, lay in it all day under a cutbank where I used to fish for catfish as a boy. I sneaked back into the ranch that night, stole a horse and saddle and headed for Texas. I made it across the Pecos and finally got to the thickets along the Rio Grande. Maverick

48

cattle live there and they'll go after a man or a horse on sight. Wart hogs run in bands and will kill a man on foot. Rattlesnakes like in every spot of shade. Outlaws who'll cut a throat for a peso or two hide out in the thicket. Law men are afraid to go in there. But Cass Irons and Zack Roper went in with Kiowa trailers and bloodhounds."

He paused exhaustedly for a moment. "They didn't get me, but they made life a hell. I got to Mexico. Cass spread word he'd pay $5000 in gold for me, dead or alive. That drove me back to the states. He found that out and put the Pinkertons on me. He doubled the reward. Ten thousand dollars and no questions asked.

"I grew this beard. I made it to Chicago, riding as a tramp on freight trains. Worked in the stockyards handling cattle for the slaughterhouses. I had shaken off the Pinkertons. I came to Wagonbow, bought up the claim on which this house stands with what money I'd managed to save. I began to feel safe. Until today when I saw Zack Roper and the others."

"Who is Zack Roper?" Jane asked.

"Range boss for Cass Irons. He got the job my father had. I saw him less than an hour ago."

"Where?"

"In town. Those two wagons you might have noticed standing in front of John Wisk's store belong to Cass Irons. Your father told me Cass himself passed through Wagonbow last summer. He's taking up ranching in Dakota Territory. Sheila Irons and little Penny were with the wagons, on their way to the new range."

"Sheila? Little Penny?"

"Sheila's the last of Cass Irons' children. Penny's a grandchild. She was Wyatt's daughter and was born after he was killed when his horse fell. Penny's mother died not long after she was born. I laid mighty low when I spotted Zack and Sheila. Maybe they wouldn't recognize me at a glance, but I didn't take any chances."

He quit talking. He was afraid to look at Jane, afraid what he might see in her face. The silence went on and on. The creaking of wheels and jingle of wagon chains drifted from the main trail. Through the window Val saw the two *Si-Si* wagons toiling past, evidently heading for the Sage Creek camp site which was less than an hour's travel beyond Val's place. Only three outriders accompanied the wagons. Zack Roper was not with them. He and the remainder of the crew were still in town, no doubt, probably enjoying the conviviality of the Golden Elk.

50

There was no sign of Sheila nor her niece. Val took it for granted they were inside the first wagon, sheltered from the wind and the dust. The spare stock passed by, hazed along by Miguel.

The wagons remained on the skyline for a time, mounting the big swell to the north. Each plodding step of the teams added that much to Val's margin of safety. In another day the *Si-Si* people should be twenty or thirty miles away. Then fifty. They would be gone out of his life once more. Chance had brought them back after eight years, reviving all the old torturing memories to bitter heat.

He had gone over it in his mind countless times. Had he really killed his friend? Was it possible there was a murder lust buried in his mind that had been released by alcohol?

He found that Jane was eying him thoughtfully. There was much in her expression now that came from her father. It was an expression he could not exactly interpret. In it was something that might have been a new respect for him as though she had come upon a phase of his character that appealed to her.

She turned and stood gazing over the crest of the swell beyond which the hoods of the two wagons were vanishing. "This

51

changes things," she finally said.

"I hoped it would not," Val said. "I never believed I could have done that terrible thing."

"But you really aren't sure?" she questioned.

Val made a gesture of hopelessness.

"I'll have to have time to think, David," she said. "Or should I address you by your real name. What was it — Valentine Lang, I believe you said?"

He did not answer that. It was over between him and Jane. He knew that. "I'll drive you back to town," he said.

"I tell you I must have time to think," she said. "You can see that."

"Of course," he said. Think? What was there for her to think about? He could not blame her. She could only go on the evidence, as Cass Irons had done. He could not believe he had killed Boone. But he could never be sure — really sure even in his own mind.

He took her arm and led her out of the house across the threshold over which he had carried her so recently in high hope, both of them laughing. He helped her into the buggy, tucked the laprobe in. He took the reins and drove into the main trail, swinging toward the stain of smoke in the sky that marked Wagonbow's location.

"You've got to give me a little time," Jane repeated desperately. "After all, this is a sudden thing."

Again he did not speak. The buggy carried them over a low rise and Wagonbow lay in sight on the flats, the setting sun casting bronze reflections from its window glass.

Coming directly toward them so near at hand there was no way of avoiding the meeting were three riders. One was Sheila Irons on a sidesaddle. At her side Penny was mounted on a miniature Spanish saddle aboard a gray burro.

It was so unexpected all Val could do was freeze in his seat. He had jumped too quickly to the conclusion that Sheila Irons had been aboard the two wagons as they had passed by. It was apparent she had remained in town to finish shopping, for she was leading a pack-mule which was slung with packages. Two hat boxes topped the load. Little Penny wore new, gold-threaded half-boots and a small jacket with a heavy fur collar.

Bringing up the rear was a leathery-faced man in a blanket coat with a flat-crowned hat which had a rawhide drawstring through its drooping brim. He was gray-templed with obsidian-dark eyes. He was Pedro

Jaguar, the Spanish-Yaqui who had been a rider for *Si-Si* for years, and whose particular duty had been as bodyguard for Sheila Irons as a child. Evidently this was still his responsibility. He rode with a Winchester slung in his arm, and a pistol outside his coat. He was scanning the washes and brush and had little interest in the occupants of the buggy, merely lifting the rifle a little in the customary salute as he passed by.

Penny stood up in the stirrups and shouted gaily, "Hi there."

Sheila also uttered a routine, "Good afternoon."

Val did not look at them directly. He lowered his head so that his hatbrim helped shield them. He uttered a gruff, "Howdy."

Then they were past. After a time he chanced a glance. They were continuing on their way, with the Yaqui still occupied in scanning the surroundings to guard against possible Indian ambush, remote as that possibility was this close to the fort.

"I take it that was this Sheila Irons and her niece," Jane said after a moment.

"Yes."

"And the Indian?"

"That was Pedo Jaguar. He's from a tribe in Mexico which some of the Conquistadores are said to have joined and which had never mixed with other people. They hold themselves above other strains in Mexico. Cass Irons rescued Pedro from Apaches when he was a small boy. Pedro, being mainly Yaqui, was grateful. When a Yaqui figures he owes you a debt like that it's for life."

"He frightened me. Did he recognize you? Or the young lady?"

"Apparently not."

"You mean you're not sure?"

"I'm sure, at least as far as Pedro is concerned. He would have killed me on the spot if he'd have known who I really was."

Jane peered back. "Well, they're almost out of sight," she said. "There's no need to worry about them. You'll never see any of them again."

3

✳✳✳✳✳✳✳✳✳✳✳✳✳✳✳✳✳✳✳✳✳✳✳✳✳✳

Jane settled back in the seat. "Now let's forget all about it and talk about something pleasant."

He looked at her, startled. "Pleasant?" he echoed. "I doubt if it's going to be that easy for either of us."

"It could be if we want it to be."

"Do you mean we're going on — as we'd planned?"

She moved closer to him. "It *is* a beautiful house," she said musingly. "Father says you've sunk more than three thousand dollars in it. That's a lot of money. I'm flattered."

Val was glad when the buildings of town loomed up in the chill dusk and she drew away from him to sit primly in the seat as he drove to the hitch lot.

"You said that the Yaqui would kill you on sight if he recognized you," she spoke. "You surely don't mean that after all this time Cass Irons still would pay ten thousand dollars for vengeance on you?"

"I'm afraid so," Val said. "But Pedro was my friend. He wouldn't kill me for money."

"For what then? Ten thousand dollars would be a fortune for a man like that. For most anyone."

"Pedro was Boone's friend also. He thinks I killed Boone. He's the one who found the marks of the corduroy in the brush, and located the bullet that had gone all the way through Boone and imbedded in a tree trunk."

She stood there for a time after he had helped her to the ground, dusk shadowing any expression in her face that might have given him a clew to her thoughts.

"Good night," she said abruptly. She did not offer her cheek for his kiss as usual.

"What comes next?" he asked.

"I don't know," she said. "We'll talk it over in a few days."

"I'm leaving in a few days for Cheyenne," he said. "I'm driving a carload of beef there to ship to Omaha. I'll be gone a week or more."

"Maybe that is best," she said. "It will give us both time to think and decide."

"Of course," he said. But he knew there was nothing to decide. It was finished.

He got his rifle from the buggy and saw her to the front door of the bank where her father, already bundled in a buffalo fur overcoat, was waiting impatiently to be driven home.

The horses belonging to Zack Roper and those of his crew who were remaining in town stood a distance down the street at the Curly Wolf bar from which came banjo music and the slap of cards and poker chips. The *Si-Si* men had moved on to fresher fields from the Golden Elk.

Val mounted and rode out of town, heading back to his own place. He rode with his mind empty. The world he had built had suddenly changed. No matter if Jane indicated that she might go on with their plans, it could never be the same between them.

It would not be fair to her. He had refused to admit that before. He did now. Each time a stranger rode up to their door, each time a cattle drive passed through the country, they would live in tension and apprehension, waiting for the moment when Cass Irons would appear with his cowboys and a hangrope on the saddlehorn.

Full darkness came. The lights of the town faded as he topped the rise. His tall house stood black and silent on its higher ground. Its walls echoed the hoofbeats of his horse as it crossed the plank bridge over the ditch that irrigated his hayfield.

The sod house was also dark and quiet, with only the faint rumor of stove smoke remaining in the air. He remembered that Benny Feather had told him he was taking Mary over to her people who were camped half a dozen miles down Beaver Creek. Mary, who was the daughter of a medicine man, did a lot of practical doctoring and nursing among her people.

Mary had left a stew on the back of the stove to be warmed, and there was coffee in the pot. He unsaddled and cared for his horse, then walked to the holding pen where he and Benny were fattening thirty head of beef cattle in preparation for marketing them at Cheyenne or shipping them over the Union Pacific to Omaha for better prices.

Upon him was the growing apathy, the feeling that he had lost all aim or target in life. From the time he had become acquainted with Jane Erskine he had seen in her the end of his loneliness, the promise of tranquility. The thought now came startlingly to him that perhaps this emotion had not been real love, only a need for companionship, a need to prove that he was a free man.

Returning to the sod house he lighted a lamp, built fire in the stove, warmed the stew and coffee. He had little appetite.

Coffee mug in hand he moved to the small kitchen window and stood gazing at the dark, sharp silhouette of the tall house. Built into it had been his dreams.

He had visualized a wife in the sewing room in the attic, with children playing there at her knee. He had imagined the beams of lamplight from the dormers, guiding him back to warmth and affection after a day on the range. Vines climbing the veranda posts in summer, the soft tones of the piano he had already ordered delivered from Omaha, laughter, the conviviality of friends and neighbors from town and other ranches.

He knew he had a reputation as a hard man to best in a trade, but he also was known as one to keep his word, win or lose. Some town people resented him for the way he had moved steadily forward. Henry Erskine was one of these, even though for the same reasons Henry would be proud to welcome him as a son-in-law.

He got a bottle from the cupboard. He drew the cork, started to slosh a drink into the empty coffee mug. He halted, put the cork back in the bottle and replaced it in the cupboard. He had not taken a drink since the night Boone Irons had been murdered. What had been drunk from the bottle had been served to visitors at the soddie. Whisky had made a wanted man of him. Whisky would not solve his problems now.

He returned to the window. But he was not seeing the black silhouette of the tall house against a rising moon that was nearly at the full. What he was seeing was Boone Irons' face. Young, handsome, vital. That had been Boone the night they had started their drinking bout. And that had been himself also. Young, reckless rakehellies trying to outdo each other. Rivals, but never enemies. They had gone through school together, had fished and hunted and faced hardship and danger on roundups side by side.

They had understood each other. Neither had a taste for whiskey and Val could not remember downing more than a second helping. How could he have been drunk enough to have murdered Boone? Even Jane believed it. He could not blame her in view of the evidence. He still had no way of knowing what devils might have been released in him by alcohol. He only knew he did not dare test those demons.

He refilled the coffee mug and continued to stand by the window, seeing everything, seeing nothing, torn by his memories and his thoughts. He kept remembering the way

Jane had accepted what he had told her. He had tried to visualize what her reaction might be. He had anticipated almost anything but the practical viewpoint she had adopted once the first moment of horror had passed.

Lantern light showed on the trail and crept nearer. Half a dozen freight wagons and smaller vehicles of travelers moved past, accompanied by a strong column of cavalry. These were arriving from the long, hard trip down the Deadwood Trail. Freighters and prospectors and stagecoaches traveled through the Sioux country only in strength now, usually escorted by troopers. The *Si-Si* wagons probably would wait over at Sage Creek until joined by more wagons heading north. That would mean that Sheila Irons and Pedro Jaguar might be traveling to and from town past his place for days until a caravan formed that would be deemed strong enough to move.

He thought of turning in but knew that sleep would be impossible, at least for hours. He had paced this room more than once in darkness through the years, scourged by the same thoughts, the same agonies of doubt and horror that beset him now. There had been times when he had almost decided to go back to New Mexico, face Cass Irons and have an end to it.

In his soul Val believed he was innocent. But he knew the stern old rancher. There would be no forgiving, no compassion in Cass. He was a product of a harsh school. He had built his own ranch in New Mexico by sheer strength and unbending will, wresting it from nature itself and from savages who tortured and raided. Cass Irons had been disciplined to live by the rule of an eye for an eye, as had his opponents.

He stood in an almost hypnotic apathy, the coffee cold in the mug, thinking, thinking endlessly. He heard riders gallop northward on the trail. He could see only their dark shadows in the moonlight, but believed he identified one as Zack Roper by his size. That would be the remainder of the *Si-Si* crew heading from town to join the wagon camp on Sage Creek.

He walked outside and headed toward the house. The night was cold and he was in shirt sleeves. He turned back and donned his heavy saddle coat and hat. On another thought, he also buckled on his six-shooter, for coyotes had been trying to raid Mary's henhouse which stood beyond the blacksmith shed.

He walked to the tall house. He had done this many times before during its construction, taking pleasure in standing among its skeleton, watching its change day by day, evening by evening, into fulfillment instead of the shadow of his dreams. The tall house had become his friend, almost a part of him. He was drawn to it now in this moment of great mental turmoil.

He unlocked the colorful door and entered the parlor. While moonlight struck through the windows. His bootheels echoed on the wooden floor. It was of cedar and he planned on soon having it waxed and gleaming with rugs to give it warmth in winter.

He climbed to the second floor, and then to the attic with its slanting, open rafters that he had left for Jane to plan and have finished as she chose. From a dormer he could see his cattle in the holding pen. The buffalo grass on the flats showed the glinting silver of frost. The sagebrush that grew stirrup high on the north slope of the rise gleamed white in the crisp night.

He threw open the casement window and let in the sharp, frosty bite of the night air. He stood looking at the beauty of it all, and the freedom whose worth he was debating. He could hear dogs barking far away. Out in the plains a coyote answered with its weird yowling.

Cass Irons was wrong. Pedro Jaguar was wrong. Jane was wrong. He could not have killed Boone. He could not give himself up to the false vengeance an embittered father would wreak on him without giving him a chance to defend himself.

He became aware of movement to the north. Shadows had appeared at the crest of the swell beyond which lay Sage Creek. They flowed over the crest, then merged with other shadows in the moonlight. They must have entered a long draw which broke the surface off to the west of the rise.

Val stood motionless, an uneasiness nudging him. Time passed. Minutes. Five. Perhaps ten. Then he saw them again. The shadows. Nearer. They were at the far end of his horse pasture, following the smooth wire fence which would bring them eventually near his ranch yard.

They were men on foot. They had left their horses somewhere and were moving in on his place. They were scattering now as they got clear of the pasture fence, winging out to encircle their objective. They were taking advantage of what cover they could find, scurrying like Indians. But they were not Indians. They wore brimmed hats. Wide-brimmed hats.

They were so close now he could make

out details. There were six of them. No, eight. One in the center of the spreading line was Zack Roper. He was giving silent orders by waving his arms and pointing. He had with him the *Si-Si* crew who had accompanied the two wagons into Wagonbow.

They were coming for him. He had been too sure that he had not been recognized that afternoon. Perhaps it had been Pedro Jaguar's keen old eyes that had penetrated the thick beard, bridged the span of eight years. Val doubted that, for, as he had told Jane, the Yaqui would have shot him down on the spot.

Then it must have been Sheila who had known who he was during that brief moment when he had passed by on the trail. No doubt she had sent a rider back to town to alert Zack Roper who would have had little trouble learning details about Val and where he could be found. That was why Roper and other *Si-Si* men had gone galloping back to Sage Creek after dark. There Zack had conferred with Sheila, then assembled the entire crew for his capture.

He crouched down, drawing the casement sash slowly closed. He peered over the sill. His presence in the tall house apparently had not been discovered. Obeying Zack's signals they were deploying past the silent, new house and spreading out to encircle the sod house on the flat below. Lamplight still burned there and they were taking it for granted that this was where they would find their quarry.

Luck had brought him to the tall house at the right time, but to be discovered meant death. That was the only thing of which he was sure. He moved to the opposite dormer to keep track of them. Zack had halted his advance a short distance from the soddie and was waiting until the encirclement was complete.

Val tiptoed downstairs and to the kitchen door at the rear of the tall house. He opened it a fraction at a time, fearing each instant that a squeak from the hinges would betray his presence and bring them upon him. But old Bill Rockwell, head carpenter on the construction of the house, was a thorough workman and the hinges had been oiled. They gave no sound.

He moved away from the house, keeping its bulk between him and the sod structure. He reached the far side of the slick-wire fence before they made their move.

Zack's deep voice sounded. "Let's go, boys! Be careful. Don't fire 'til I give the word. An' don't shoot each other!"

The rush of bootheels sounded as they

charged upon the soddie. However, some excited cowboy started shooting. The others must have thought that it was Zack who had opened up, for other guns began booming. Val could hear glass in the windows shattering.

He ran at full speed, reaching cover of thin brush beyond his ranch clearing. He followed this until he entered a small dry wash that came steeply off the big swell over which he had first sighted them approaching.

Apparently the *Si-Si* men were in confusion. There was wild shouting and new bursts of gunfire, with Zack Roper howling questions and shouting conflicting orders.

Val raced up the wash. He believed the *Si-Si* men must have left their horses in this gully. If so they were still uphill from him, for he could see no hoofmarks in the sandy underfooting.

He kept running. Finally he heard horses stirring ahead. He slowed, fearing he might spook them. The animals loomed up suddenly close at hand in the moonlight. He was taking it for granted they had been left picketed, and that Zack had taken the entire crew with him to surround the sod house.

He was mistaken. A figure arose in his path. His first thought was that it was one of the Negro mule skinners. He dove forward instantly, taking his quarry at the knees.

The person he hurled jarringly to the ground was a woman! Sheila Irons! He realized this in time to halt the blow from his clenched fist that he had intended for his victim.

He rolled clear. "Sheila!" he panted. "I didn't know it was you!"

He felt sure she was no more than stunned momentarily for he had seen displays of how supple and resilient was that deceptively slim figure.

He arose and ran among the horses. Roper's black mount, the biggest of the lot, bore a fine, hand-carved saddle. It was double-rigged, with a short rope tied to the horn, Texas style. Many of the riders from the *Si-Si* preferred the longer lariat, Spanish and California-style, but Zack Roper had always been a tie-down man. He liked to upend cattle when they would not heed his will. He weighed two hundred and ten pounds and always cut the best and biggest mounts into his own string. There was a rifle in the boot on the saddle. Zack never had been much of a rifleshot. He had always preferred to come to close quarters with a six-shooter even against game that was difficult to corner. As far as Val knew Zack had never been called on to draw a gun against a man, but the *Si-Si* range boss often carried a brace of six-shooters when in town on payday, an affectation that was an invitation to anyone who considered himself tough enough to test him. Nobody had ever tried to determine just how good he was with a pistol.

Sheila was sitting up, still gasping. She had a pistol in her hand, but Val seized it from her and tossed it off into the darkness. She wore a heavy duck saddle coat and a divided riding skirt. A scarf was tied over her hair.

"You — you — murderer!" she choked.

Val freed the remaining horses from their tethers and stampeded them away into the brush. He mounted the black horse and hazed the loose animals into greater panic.

Sheila had got to her feet and was frenziedly scrambling through the clumps of grass in search of her gun which he had tossed away. He knew she would shoot him if she found it.

He rode away up the shallow draw. Presently he swung the black horse out of the draw and headed across the open plain in the cold moonlight.

The red glow of fire began to rise above the swells behind him. It grew in volume until he could see soaring spears of flame. There was only one object in that direction that would create a blaze of that magnitude. The tall house. Zack, when he found that his quarry had slipped through his fingers, had vented his fury on the only object at hand. The tall house, which had never been occupied, was the victim.

The glare grew until it filled the sky to the south. The tall house was being consumed, just as his dreams were consumed. He could picture what else was happening. He knew Zack's capacity for savage violence when he was enraged. No doubt the sod house was also being wrecked, and burned.

He could only guess at the fate of his horses and cattle. At best Zack would probably turn them out on the range to be rustled or become mavericks. The chances were he would slaughter them on the spot.

Sheila's words, and their horror and contempt, kept echoing in his memory. "You — you — murderer!"

A beard and eight years had not been enough to disguise him from her eyes. Now her father would be after him again. It was starting all over, the game of hide and backtrack, of sleeping always lightly with a saddled horse at hand or skulking in outlaw hangouts, never free to tell his true identity

71

to anyone, to other hunted men least of all, for they were the kind to be first to claim the reward on his head if given the chance.

His thoughts swung to Jane Erskine. The decision had been made with brutal finality for both of them. The chances were they would never see each other again. He wondered if Jane would grieve, and for how long? No doubt she would feel the sting of barbed tongues and be the victim of condescending, cold smiles at the hands of townspeople, particularly the women, who would enjoy humiliating her for her narrow escape from marrying a man wanted for murder.

He kept riding. The glow began to fade in the sky. By this time, no doubt, Zack and the *Si-Si* men would have rounded up the stampeded mounts and be riding in the hope of cutting his trail.

He had some advantages. He knew the country better than they, at least south of Red Buttes. More than that, he had experience at this game. He knew the sad art of staying ahead of pursuit, of circle and back circle, of putting himself in their place and deciding what he would do if their positions were reversed, then doing the opposite.

4

✳✳✳✳✳✳✳✳✳✳✳✳✳✳✳✳✳✳✳✳✳✳✳✳✳

He avoided the wagon trail, but kept it to his left. He followed a stretch of sandy country over which a sharp wind was droning. After a time he veered back into the trail itself, gambling that the wind would blur the tracks of the horse in the sand so that even Pedro Jaguar would not know he had passed this way.

Army pack trains and probably a freight string or two would be sure to pass along the wagon road early in the morning and grind out all traces of his own use of the road. But, most of all, he was counting on them expecting him to head south toward the Platte and the Union Pacific Railroad.

He had used railroads in the past to elude the Pinkertons and carry him to populated areas where they had been unable to pick up trace of him. They would put the Pinkertons on him again. Zack Roper would see to that as soon as he could get to the telegraph office at Wagonbow. The professional detectives would study the history of his previous flight from them and would expect him to follow that same pattern.

This time he meant to avoid civilization and head into the Sioux country. That offered the risk of not only death, but torture, but if he made it there were the mining camps of the Dakota Black Hills that could be reached. The law was weak there, and he also had the upper Missouri River country as refuge, with even Canada or the Pacific Coast as possibilities.

He had risked riding beyond Red Buttes only a time or two on hunting trips alone. He had encountered no Indians, but had not been in the country long enough to pick up more than a hazy idea of the terrain. He had gained additional information from talking to old-time trappers, a few of whom lived in Wagonbow, and from Benny and Mary Feather whose people hunted buffalo at times north of the buttes.

The main impression he had was that down in New Mexico the country would have been termed *muy malo* or *malpais,* which meant that it was very bad and very rough country.

Few white men dared to travel it now that the trapping breed was almost extinct. Buffalo existed there in great numbers. The so-called southern herd of buffalo, whose habitat was from the Platte River south across the Arkansas into the Staked Plains, had been about wiped out after a dozen years of relentless hunting since the Civil War.

The Kansas Pacific Railroad and the Sante Fe had made the task of the hide hunters easier in that area. The army had also cooperated by establishing forts to subdue the tribes and by encouraging hunters to eliminate the Indians' commissary — the buffalo. Shipping "flints," as the dried hides were called, along with smoked tongues and jerky to eastern markets had been made relatively easy.

There were few roads north of the Platte Valley, along which the Union Pacific Railroad had been built after the war, and no railroads at all. The few army forts that held out along the Deadwood Trail were under almost constant alert.

While game should be easy to bring down in that country he would need other necessities of life. Blankets for one, and ammunition. The rifle Roper had left on his saddle was a .44-40, the workhorse gun of cattlemen because shells could be used from the six-shooter in case of shortage. There were five cartridges in the rifle and five in his own side gun, which, as usual, carried an empty under the firing pin.

He debated ways of acquiring what he would need. He even considered heading for the *Si-Si* wagons that would be camped on Sage Creek and raiding them for supplies. But the chances were that the two Negro mule skinners would be on guard there. He had little other choice.

He headed east across the open flats toward the sod house Ed Blake had built on the homestead on Antelope Fork. The distance was five miles. The claim now, in effect, belonged to Val, although the final transfer of ownership would not be complete until the papers were filed with the court.

Daybreak was not far away when he dismounted and pounded on the slab door of the place. It was Ed's voice, thick with sleep, that responded. Ed, gun in hand, opened the door after making doubly sure of the identity of his visitor.

"What'n blazes!" he exclaimed. "What's wrong, Val?"

"Glad I found you still here," Val said. "I was afraid you might have pulled out last night."

"It'll be a day or two before we can git goin'," Ed said, puzzled. "Now why — ?"

"I'd like to buy a blanket or two," Val said.

"And a bed tarp. Some flour and salt and a few other items of grub if you can spare any. Some .44s."

His wallet was in his coat, he had it in his hand and began pulling out gold coins.

He blocked the question that was on Ed's lips. "If anyone comes this way to ask about me, tell them I put a gun in your face and took what I wanted. Tell them you don't know which way I headed."

Ed asked no questions. He made sure the windows were blinded, then lighted a lamp. His wife, a wrapper over her nightdress, peered from the sleeping room but he harshly ordered her to go back to bed and told her she had neither seen nor heard anything.

Ed got together a pack that included flour, a bag of venison jerky, coffee, beans, salt and baking powder and half a dozen cans of vegetables.

His wife, disobeying orders to stay out of it, brought blankets and a quilt — from their own bed, Val surmised. Ed added a wagontarp to the collection and Alice Blake got together a skillet, coffeepot, two tin plates and a cook pot, along with forks and spoons.

"You'll find use for this too," Ed said, handing Val a skinning knife. "But I've got

no .44s. All I got is an old .45-70 Springfield."

He tried to refuse the goldpieces Val
forced on him. "Mind what I tell you about
saying I took this stuff at gunpoint, in case
anyone comes along," Val warned him.
"Don't get mixed up in this. Get out of the
country as soon as you can."

They shook hands. "You always treated us
like human bein's," Ed said. "I don't know
what this is all about an' don't want to know.
But what about your place? Your cattle?
Your new house? The one you was buildin'
for Jane Erskine?"

"So long," Val said.

He rode away. Daybreak was on the plains
to the east. An overcast that had the lifeless
pallor of a shroud, had moved in. A bitter
wind fingered through the frozen grass.

A cold object struck his cheek. A snow-
flake. More came. Soon he could see no
more than a hundred yards as the storm increased. He kept the cutbanks of the Antelope Fork to his right, knowing that its
course was north and south for half a dozen
more miles.

The snow came in a white flood. At least
he no longer had to worry about blinding his
trail. He let the horse set its own pace
against the storm. He judged it was about

noon when he threw off in the lee of boulders. The wind had swept an area of snow down to the roots of the grama and he let the black horse rustle on picket while he gnawed at the jerky Ed Blake had supplied.

He continued to ride northward into the storm. At midafternoon he saw the line of bluffs ahead and before twilight came he had worked the tired horse up through boulder-strewn talus into a defile where he had shelter from the wind and a dry camp beneath the overhang of a rock wall.

He managed to find enough dry twigs and grass lodged under the cliffs to start a fire. He dragged in more fuel to dry and with which to replenish the fire. With the storm still howling across the flats there was little chance his fire would be detected. From past experience he knew there would likely be many times in the future when he could not afford such a risk. Therefore he took advantage of being as comfortable as possible at the moment.

The storm blew for nearly two days. As was often the case at this early season the temperatures were not unduly severe, but snow piled deep in the defile and formed great drifts on the flats.

Val and the horse were nearly walled in by the downfall. During lulls he tramped an exit from their shelter and located small areas of wind-swept flats where the horse could paw for grazing.

He turned out at dawn to find the sky clearing. He boiled coffee, heated food and let the fire die. His reprieve was over. The snow that had been his ally, shielding him from pursuit, could now become an enemy. Any trail made by a horse and rider could be spotted for long distances in this white-clad land by any observer on a vantage point. And he was sure there would be such watchers before long, now that travel was again possible on the flats.

Every instinct was to saddle up and put more distance between himself and Wagon-bow. Sober reasoning ruled that out. A running man, even when conditions were in his favor, was always easier to see than a hidden man. He decided to remain where he was, for the time at least. He located more grazing for the horse, then led it back to hiding in the defile.

The sun came out in a blue sky. Snow crackled underfoot. The temperature soon began to climb. The cliffs sparkled in the sun and reflected rainbow hues into the cleft. Carrying the rifle, he climbed to a high ridge. This gave him a view for miles south across the white surface of the flats. In the clear air he could make out the pale, dark haze that marked the smoke rising from the stove fires of Wagonbow. The location of his own spread was hidden by the rolling land west of town. For that he was thankful. He knew that all he might have seen was a black scar.

The flats offered only a blank face for two or three hours. He grew cold and had to flex arms and legs to offset the chill, even though the temperature had climbed above freezing. The snow was softening already. Blobs began to plop from the trees and brush, and small slides plunged from the faces of the ridges.

It was past midmorning, according to the position of the sun, when he saw the first sign of movement. The wood detail moved along the Deadwood Trail from the fort, reinforced by a detachment with shovels and fresno scrapers to clear the drifts. They would travel no farther than Sage Creek where there was timber.

After a time horsemen appeared on the open flats. Three riders. They were having heavy going in the drifts and finally halted. Two presently turned back, heading in the direction of Wagonbow. One of these was a bigger man than the other. Val believed he was Zack Roper, although, at that distance, it was impossible to be certain.

The third rider continued to make his way toward the bluffs taking a tortuous route to avoid the heavier drifts. His course would bring him to the bluffs nearly two miles west of Val's position. Val guessed it would be Pedro Jaguar, who had drawn this task because of his keen eyesight and experience as a trailer.

As the horseman worked his way nearer the bluffs Val saw that his guess had been right. It was the Yaqui. Pedro Jaguar was famous for his skill at ferreting out wary old steers that had evaded other roundup riders. He had also, a time or two, tracked down criminals for the law, but on those occasions the men he had helped bring to bay had committed particularly heinous crimes.

Pedro finally vanished among the boulders and gullies at the foot of the bluffs to the west. Val made sure his own lookout point was not visible from that direction no matter what ridge the Yaqui selected for his peering.

The draw that served as Val's base was in sight below his own position and the snow there was marked by the trails he had made. It was impossible to cover those signs of his presence, but there were not too many points from which a man could look down into the defile. He could only hope that Pedro did not scout eastward along the rims.

He believed he had gained one point on which he had counted — a big point — in his favor. The fact that Zack had turned back to Wagonbow — and he was certain now it had been Zack — could mean that the *Si-Si* range boss felt that Val was far more likely to head south than into the Sioux country. The fact he was stationing only one man to the north seemed to bear out this belief.

This hope was strengthened during the afternoon. Riders appeared off to the south at intervals, but soon faded into the roll of the country. None continued northward toward the bluffs. From the numbers he sighted he realized that posses were being organized and the country was being scanned both east and west of town — and probably in greater strength southward. Even though the snow was softening, it would be hard going for both men and mounts and only a big goal would induce posses to ride with any enthusiasm under the conditions. A goal of say $10,000.

Evidently Pedro Jaguar was equipped to spend the night in the bluffs, for sundown came and there was no sign of him heading back to town. The temperature still climbed. A chinook was setting in. Black areas of open ground began to show on the flats.

Val returned to his camp. He did not dare build a fire, for he had no way of knowing whether the Yaqui might be near or far away. The tang of woodsmoke would no longer be dissipated by high winds and snow and he knew how surprisingly far it could be detected. Pedro's perceptions in such matters were far keener than that of the average hunter.

He did not sleep soundly. He came rigidly awake time after time and lay listening. But he always decided it had been the sloshy sound of melting snow falling from timber or cliffs. Water was now running in the draw, chuckling and gurgling. The chinook, damp and raw, was blowing steadily, erasing the snow of winter's first storm.

The chinook lingered all the next day. Toward late afternoon he sighted Pedro Jaguar heading away from the base of the bluffs toward Wagonbow. By that time all that remained of the snow were fading patches of gray-white on the flats that was turning into an ocean of mud.

Evidently the Yaqui had decided that further vigil in that direction was wasted time.

Val felt a trifle easier in mind. If it was true that Pedro was returning to Wagonbow, it meant he could leave his hiding place and resume his journey north, putting more miles between himself and the hunters.

He had been grimly afraid of Pedro and his genius for following a trail where there was nothing for other men to see. He could never use a rifle on Pedro. The old Yaqui had been guide and counselor to both Val and Boone Irons from boyhood. Pedro had taught them not only the finer points of handling a lariat and the science of judging cattle, but had tried to impart to them what he could of tracking game. He had shown them how to live off the country, how to build a fire without matches, where to find edible plants and fruits in what seemed to be barren desert.

Pedro, however, would have nothing to do in helping them in the use of firearms. He was a deadly rifleshot himself, but said that as far as hunting game for food went, any fool could aim a gun that well. Val had sometimes wondered whether Pedro, who had once told them his father had the power of black magic and foresight, might have inherited that trait and had foreseen that he or Boone were to die by a bullet in the future.

He had no illusions. Pedro had never

shown favoritism between him and Boone. He had settled their hotheaded squabblings, yanking them apart at times when they had clenched their all-too-ready fists, letting them punch at each other at other times. Either way his decisions had turned out to have been right at those particular moments. He had been unswerving in his views of right and wrong. In the matter of Boone's murderer he would be an implacable executioner if he believed it necessary. In any event he would do his best to take Val to Cass Irons alive. If it had been the other way around, and Boone was the wanted man, with Val the victim, he was sure Pedro would be as relentless in pursuit of the one he considered guilty.

Val decided to linger one more day in his hideout, spending the hours after dawn on his lookout. The chinook now brought cold rain that dissipated the last of the snowdrifts. Every stream came to life and the flats were bogs. He huddled beneath the tarp and watched what movement there was to the south.

Cavalry patrols rode out from the fort, scouting up the trail as far as the bluffs, but always returning to the post by nightfall. Routine procedure. The woodtrain made its daily trip to Sage Creek and back.

One cavalry patrol skirted the base of the bluffs almost to Val's position. They were accompanied by Crows and civilian scouts who scanned the area for sign. He did not believe they were looking for him. They were making sure no raiding parties of Sioux had come south of the bluffs. They finally swung back to the fort by way of town. Their attitudes showed boredom.

He sighted more posses. If any rode as far as Ed Blake's homestead on Antelope Fork, Val did not detect it. He suspected that Ed and his family had lost no time after his visit in packing up what few belongings they had and heading for Cheyenne to board a train for more hospitable country.

The fact that searchers did not approach the bluffs continued to indicate that the hunt must still be concentrated to the south in the direction of the transcontinental railroad.

On the fourth morning of his concealment he saw two wagons pulling out of the Sage Creek timber and moving up the Deadwood Trail. The rain had ended. A cold wind was setting in, drying the country and beginning to harden the flats and the road.

There were the two *Si-Si* wagons. He became certain of that after studying them for a while. He was in doubt at first because they seemed to be flanked by only three riders. There was a wrangler bringing up the rear with the remuda, and that would be Miguel. One of the riders was feminine. Sheila Irons. He saw no sign of her small niece, but Penny was in the lead wagon, no doubt, taking shelter from the raw wind.

Val watched, frowning. The two riders had the drivers and Miguel to help in case trouble came, and the chance of danger was remote south of the buttes, but he could not understand why Zack was exposing Cass Irons' daughter and granddaughter to even the remote possibility of anything happening.

The wagons vanished among low ridges through which the Deadwood Trail wound far to the west and he reasoned that they would soon camp in that area for the night. Zack evidently was holding over with the others in Wagonbow to continue the manhunt. No doubt he and his men would overtake the wagons before they proceeded beyond the bluffs.

Even so it was a dubious decision on Zack's part. There had been no raids on the trail south of Red Buttes in two or three years, but that was no assurance that a raiding party might not chance it again in spite of the proximity to the cavalry post.

Val broke camp the next morning. He climbed to a lookout for a final survey southward. The wood train was moving out from the fort. A freighter was pulling out of Wagonbow, heading for the Sage Creek camp grounds. There was no sign of the *Si-Si* wagons on the Deadwood Trail to the west. No doubt Zack and the rest of his men had rejoined the wagons during the night and they were proceeding north.

Val returned and loaded his camppack on the black horse. He was already beginning to ration what the Blakes had given him. From now on he would have to live mainly off the country. He had sighted antelope several times during his vigil on the ridge. Some had come within range, but he had not dared fire a shot that might bring company he did not want.

Always in his mind was the picture of the granite-hard face and keen eyes of Pedro Jaguar. The abandonment of vigil on the bluffs might have only been a ruse on Pedro's part to lull his quarry into false security. The Yaqui might have returned under cover of darkness and be on some vantage point, waiting, peering.

Val traveled slowly, carefully, traveling the rough, brush-tangled bottoms of ravines and gullies whenever possible. He dismounted often to make his way to an elevation and peer for sight of pursuit. All he saw was the loneliness of the wild land into which he was working his way deeper.

Open flats appeared ahead at last at mid-afternoon, offering easy going, but also greater chance of discovery. He waited until deep twilight before venturing into them. A faint moon was in the sky, but it was often completely obscured by clouds.

However, his mount proved to be an excellent night horse with that sense of depth and direction that is not the gift of the average saddle animal. Zack Roper, of course, had picked it for this trait, as well as its stamina when cutting it into his string from the *Si-Si* remuda.

Val began to find kinship between himself and the powerful black horse. Zack had always been tough on his mounts, more inclined to use the quirt than patience, often working them beyond their limit.

The black seemed to expect the same kind of treatment at Val's hands and when it did not come it moved along willingly, its ears no longer pinned back, a spring in its step. At heart it proved to be gentle and in need of companionship. Val tried to spread his bed tarp near where it grazed and kept it picketed close to his bed at night.

He camped at dawn and resumed his journey at twilight. He held a northward course, but he had again entered rough country with ridges often blocking the way, forcing long detours. When dawn came he shot an antelope that he cooked over fast-burning twigs in a ravine. Even Pedro Jaguar's eyes could hardly have detected that faint smear of smoke at a distance.

Afterward he sat by the coals for a time, taking advantage of the fading warmth. Up to this point all his actions had been those of immediate self-preservation. Now, reasonably safe from pursuit, he began to take a long look at his situation and to appraise and plan his future.

It was not a bright prospect. If Cass Irons followed his methods of the past every law officer in the West would again have new reward posters bearing his picture and description.

Except for two army forts there were no settlements for many days travel ahead until the Black Hills were reached. Prospectors had stampeded into the hills after Custer had announced discovery of gold there a few years earlier. Deadwood was said to contain more than a thousand people and many of them were rumored to be outlaws and wanted men. Farther west, along the

Yellowstone, cattlemen like Cass Irons were moving in with big crews of heavily armed fighting men to found new fortunes.

He decided to try for Deadwood first. He got a wavery look at himself in the surface of a pool along a stream. Already he was taking on the hunted look of a wild thing. His beard, which he had kept immaculate in the past, had grown matted and unkempt. His hands and face were blackened by camp smoke.

He shuddered. He had seen ragged, half-savage white men who appeared occasionally in Wagonbow, traded furs for supplies and ammunition, then vanished into the plains again. Nobody questioned them, nobody followed them, nobody knew their names. And did not care. No doubt they too had fled into the wilds as fugitives and had sunk into semi-savagery. Some had become squawmen and had joined with the Indians as renegades, others were hermits who avoided all other humans and lived in squalor as an animal lives.

Val sat tight-lipped, grim-eyed. He would not let them drive him to that. Not Cass Irons. Not Sheila Irons. Nor Zack Roper.

He whetted the skinning knife the Blakes had given him and sawed off his beard until all that was left was a ragged film of his lean jaws. He longed for a razor. He stripped and endured the cleansing agony of a swift bath in the icy stream. He heaped wood on the fire and stood there rubbing himself dry until he felt alive again — and rejuvenated.

He drowned out the fire and settled down to sleep. He dropped off instantly, putting aside his future course beyond Deadwood until Deadwood was a reality and not only an objective of the moment.

And then the decision was made for him. He awakened suddenly and lay taut and listening. His horse had aroused also. The animal's ears were pricked and its nostrils were conning the air for sound. The sun was up, but its rays were just touching the rims of the bluffs. He could have been asleep only a few minutes.

There was sound somewhere in these badlands, but it was not near enough to be an immediate danger to him. It was so faint, so indefinite that, at first, he believed it might have been made by coyotes far away.

Then something inside him went cold and his stomach began to crawl. These were not animal sounds. They were human sounds. Inhuman sounds rather. Suddenly he knew that what he was hearing was the ululation of savage voices, of warriors, of men killing other men. Faint heavy undertones were the reports of rifles.

5

****

The chilling, elusive sound faded and died.
The morning was silent again. Whatever had
happened — wherever it had happened, it
was over.

Val rolled out of his blankets and donned
his boots and saddle coat. Despite the sun-
light the day was turning colder. His bootheels grated on frozen ground. Ice crackled
at the margin of the stream. He climbed to a
rise which gave him a wider view.

He lay there for a long time, the cold
working into him. He had seen a band of antelope bounding away at a considerable distance to the northwest. The Deadwood
Trail must lay in that direction, hidden by
the ridges. After a time, and not as far away,
a pair of gray wolves appeared briefly, running as though eluding something, and vanished.

Mounted figures appeared briefly, crossing a flat. They were Indians, blanket-
wrapped and pushing their ponies at a lope.

They drove loose stock ahead of them, and some appeared to be carrying packs. They were swallowed again by the hills before he could make an accurate count of their numbers, but there were at least twenty of them.

He waited five minutes more and sighted the Indians once more. They were traveling steadily east. Otherwise the country remained vacant.

He returned to his camp, packed, saddled and headed west, keeping to cover. After a mile he began getting glimpses of the wagon trail between ridges and bluffs. It coiled through the rough country, skirting bluffs and boulders which bulged through the surface like giant monuments. It was an area where an ambush could have been mounted in a score of places. But only silence prevailed, and what portions of the road he could see remained vacant.

He dismounted and moved on hands and knees to the final rise overlooking the road. He crouched there, staring for seconds, a sickness growing in him.

The two *Si-Si* wagons were the ones that had been hit. He arose and forced himself to walk down the slope and among the silent scene of past carnage. The bodies of two men lay a little apart from the wagons. Evidently they had been shot down as the wagons drew abreast of the ambush in which the Indians awaited.

One was a stranger to him, but the other was Shorty Long. Or had been. The mutilated, scalped body was not easy to recognize. From the looks they hadn't had a chance to fight back.

The bodies of the two Negro drivers lay among the carcasses of slain mules that had been shot down in harness. There was evidence they had put up a fight, for there were empty cartridges around them. Their bodies had not been touched after death by the Indians.

Miguel Ortez had tried to escape. He had been overtaken alive and his fate had been the worst of all. He would never thrum his mandolin again and Shorty Long would not again play a jig at roundup wagons on his harmonica.

The mules had all been shot, and hunks of meat had been knifed from some of them — probably while still alive in some cases. The carcasses of two horses lay among the slain stock, but the others had been taken by the Indians who looked down on mules as beasts for inferiors.

Val moved in a daze of horror. But where were the others? Zack, Pedro Jaguar? There should be six more, in all. There had been eight riders flanking the wagons the day he saw them pass by on the street at Wagon-bow.

And Sheila and the child? He forced himself to look inside the wagon where Sheila and Penny Irons would have been riding if they had been along.

Bracing himself to face more horror, he mounted over the hub and seat of the nearest wagon. It contained only furniture and boxes and bales of supplies. He moved to the second wagon. The sun gave the hood a golden glow, the weather cracks forming patterns that changed eerily as the cold morning wind fingered the canvas.

A gay Mexican blanket had been hung inside the front bow to give privacy to Sheila and the child. It was torn partly from its hangings. Two pallets had been arranged in the wagon on bunk frames, one above the other.

The beds were empty. Quilts and blankets were strewn around. A great, square trunk, with a mirror inside its lid, had been over-turned and its contents yanked out. What was left had been trampled by moccasined feet. A bloody hand had smeared the mirror.

There was more blood on the cedar plank that served as a seat in the bow of the wagon. A wisp of nut-brown hair, fine of texture, was caught where the plank met the rough boards of the wagon's side. That would be the child's hair.

He leaped from the vehicle. Scanning the area he found the print of a young woman's bare foot in softer earth where the sun had thawed the surface. Sheila Irons. Both of them, then, had been taken away by the raiders. They had been alive at least. But for how long? Children, especially girls, usually were not permitted to live long as captives in the hands of hostiles. Sheila might be allowed to linger for a day or two longer against her will.

Possibly one or both had been wounded, but Val doubted that. He believed it was more likely the bloodstains he had found in the wagon had come from the hands of the mutilators of the dead.

Some of the *Si-Si* horses that had been run off had been shod and their trail was easy to follow. The raiders had headed toward the rough country to the northeast and the Indians he had sighted earlier riding in that direction were the guilty ones beyond a doubt.

He stood among the bodies of the dead. Shorty Long, Miguel and the other rider apparently had been riddled with bullets and arrows from ambush before they could fire a gun. The empty shells around the two Negro drivers indicated that they might have taken some of their attackers with them into death. If so, the Indians had taken away their wounded or dead.

Val's first thought was that these men must have some sort of burial. It seemed indecent to have to let them lie here. Along with that came fury at the indignities that had been inflicted on them. There was the question as to how this monstrous thing had been allowed to take place. Why hadn't Zack Roper and the rest of the *Si-Si* crew been here? The chances were that the Indians would never have jumped so strong a party.

Why had the two wagons continued up the trail beyond Red Buttes instead of waiting for the full crew to arrive? The thought struck him that Zack and the others might be dead also. They might have been ambushed, too, before they caught up with the wagons. But that didn't answer the question as to why Sheila and the child had gone ahead with the wagons.

He had no tools for burying these men in the frozen, rocky ground. And, indeed, no time. Sooner or later an army patrol or a freight string would come along the trail and find the looted wagons and the dead.

The cavalry would probably go through the usual gesture of organizing a scouting company to try to find the guilty Indians. That would mean days of delay, for Fort Miles was nearly a hundred miles away. By that time the captives would be dead or would have vanished into the nomadic world of the Sioux or Cheyennes whose villages were always on the move across the vastness of the plains.

His duty, regardless of the murder charge, was to the living. Sheila and the child might still be alive. He had known Sheila from childhood. After he had grown up enough to draw pay as a full-fledged riding hand on the C-Bar-C he bought her the prettiest doll he could find each Christmas until she finally made it plain that she was growing up also and could no longer accept such juvenile presents from a friend.

She had been fourteen when she had laid down the law to him. He had been bewildered by her anger that day. She had called him a blind, stupid idiot. Up to that time he had looked on her as he would a boy, what with her riding roundup whenever she wasn't away at school, her shrill, excited yipping when the chase for steers or calves was on. He had teased her from babyhood, pulled her pigtails.

He was now remembering her as he had seen her eight years later in Wagonbow, a shapely, strikingly handsome young woman, poised and mature. And he remembered the horror and scorn with which she had looked at him the night he had hurled her to the ground when he was escaping from Zack. He would never forget her words: "You — you — murderer!"

A new storm was brewing. An overcast had moved in. The sky was low and lifeless. A sound caused him to whirl, lifting his rifle. Like a spirit rising from the grave, one of the mules was struggling to its feet from among the carcasses of its companions.

It stood quivering, its head sagging, still tangled in harness. It had two bullet wounds, but they appeared to have been glancing shots. One had plowed a furrow near the spinal cord and this had stunned the animal. Val freed it from the harness and doctored the injuries with axle grease from the buckets that hung on the reaches of the wagons. Its trembling ceased.

He searched among the looted wagons, salvaged a sack of flour, a side of bacon, salt and a dozen or more tins of vegetables. These he loaded on the mule, along with more quilts, blankets and a wagonsheet.

He could find no weapons on the slain

men. Evidently they had all been taken by the Indians who had also stripped the bodies of three of the men of all clothing.

On a hunch he climbed into the wagon, delved beneath the pallets and found a loaded, short-muzzled .38 pistol, along with a box of shells. That evidently had been Sheila's pallet, and the fact the gun had not been fired indicated how complete the surprise of the attack had been.

The heavy wool riding stockings and boots that Sheila and little Penny had worn lay in the litter on the floor. He added the footwear to the pack on the mule along with several garments that he salvaged from the chaos.

Lashing the pack on the mule, he then led it to where the black horse waited, mounted and headed away on the trail of the raiders.

It was easy to follow. The Indians had made no attempt to hide it. They apparently felt they were safe because of the distance from the fort at Wagonbow. Indeed, events of the summer had proved that any military force venturing into this area was risking the fate that had befallen Custer.

In addition, if the new storm broke, there would be no trail to follow. The wind carried the increasing threat of snow. A gray haze had blotted out the hills to the west.

Snow was already falling there and the storm was moving steadily eastward.

He crowded the black horse to a faster pace. The mule was unwilling for a time, not being accustomed to working on a hackamore and a lead rope, but finally settled down to the jogging gait.

The trail was now more than three hours old, but it began to freshen. The war party evidently was not in a hurry, and was burdened by loot and the stolen horses. Val was not the expert at reading sign that was Pedro Jaguar but the lessons the Yaqui had taught him were valuable now.

The Indians had stopped to build a fire and eat after riding about five miles from the scene of the massacre. The fare probably had been mule meat, for Val found chunks of it abandoned, scorched and raw. Evidently the Indians were in no need of food, for there surely must be buffalo to be had for the hunting.

But more valuable than this find was the single track of a small foot he came upon in a patch of old, soft snow. Penny's foot, for surely there would be no small children with a war party. Apparently it had been bound in cloth of some kind as protection from the cold. Only Sheila would do that, for Indians would care nothing about the misery of a captive, particularly a young, helpless female.

They were both still alive, then. At least they had been little more than two hours earlier. He slowed his pace, realizing that he might be gaining too rapidly and be discovered. In that case, the Indians would set an ambush for him. Worse yet, they might kill the captives so as to have no criminal evidence around in case Val was the forerunner of a larger party of pursuers. All he could do was to hope to trail them to their first night camp. And then . . . ? Just what he could do against a score of them he had no idea.

He approached each rise carefully, peering ahead on foot before bringing the animals up. Always there was that chill inside him. Always he was expecting ambush, the whine of an arrow, the impact of a bullet. He was alert to every movement, every sway of a twig, every movement of the ears of the black horse and the mule. He was depending on them to warn him of danger that might be beyond the ability of his own senses to detect.

But the real terror in his mind was from another source. At each turn in the trail he expected to find the bodies of Sheila or Penny, or both. But the Indians continued to let the captives live.

Then the trail forked into three segments. Val had anticipated something like this, and had dreaded it. He knew it was customary Indian strategy. His problem now was to decide which of the three parties the captives were with. And there was the still more bitter possibility that Sheila and the child had been separated.

He dismounted and walked for considerable distances along each of the three trails which fanned out in directions that would carry them many miles apart into a labyrinth of buttes and ridges to the north. He scanned the frozen ground, what brush there was, the rocks, hoping for some clew — another strand of Sheila's hair, or Penny's, such as he had found at the wagons. A thread, a scrap torn from their garments to show the way. He found nothing.

He returned to the point where the trail had split, shaken by the problem, knowing that there could be no recovery from a wrong guess.

It was while he stood there that he realized that he was being watched. Perhaps it was the actions of the black horse or the mule that had warned him. Or he might have heard a slight sound.

He took it for granted that he had walked into the ambush by the Indians that he had feared all day. He dropped instantly flat, rolling over and bringing the rifle into readiness.

"No! No!" a deep voice said. "Do not shoot! There is no need for that at this time!"

The voice was that of the Spanish-Yaqui, Pedro Jaguar.

"Remain still, señor!" Pedro said. "I do not intend to kill you unless you want it so. Do not turn or look in this direction. I will shoot if you insist."

He heard Pedro slide down a boulder from a hiding place and move up behind him. Pedro took the rifle from his hand, prodded him to his feet and lifted the pistol from his holster.

"You may now face me Señor Val," Pedro said. He had been educated by the padres at Santa Fe and while each word still carried an accent that no one had ever been able to exactly imitate, he was proud of his command of English. However, at times, under stress, he lapsed into less stilted diction.

"You have been very careless," Pedro said critically. "You have forgotten many of the things I taught you. A dozen times, yes, if you had looked back at the right time, you would have discovered me following you. Did I not warn you to always make sure you know where you have come from as well as where you are going? Therefore you will never be lost when you return."

"I didn't expect to return," Val said. "And this time, I was more interested in what was ahead than what was back of me. Well, you've got me. Now what?"

"That I do not know immediately. You are not the one I want at this time. If I shoot you, the sound might warn those I am anxious to overtake."

"Such as a pack of warriors who seem to have Sheila Irons and the little girl with them."

"That is so."

"What are they, Cheyennes or Sioux?"

"I do not know for sure. I can only guess. I think they must be Sioux."

"How long have you been following me?"

"I arrived at the wagons not long after you had left. I sighted you far away."

"You don't mean you're alone?"

"I am alone, unfortunately. I decided the Señor Zack was wrong in letting the senorita and the *muchacha* proceed so far with so few *vaqueros* to guard them. I left Wagonbow with a pack animal to overtake them."

"You mean Zack and the rest of them are still back there? In Wagonbow?"

"That is so. There or thereabouts. He is still looking for you. He thought it best to send the wagons through to this Fort Steele where *el patrón* has established the new *rancho*. He was informed there was no danger from the savages."

"No danger? From the Indians? Who told him that?"

"The *soldados* at the military post. *El coronel* himself."

"Then the soldiers and the colonel must have been drunk."

"Señor Zack was told the treaty had been recently signed and the savages had agreed to return to reservation."

"Somebody heard wrong," Val said. "And they're getting farther ahead every minute while we palaver. They've split up into at least three bunches."

Pedro studied him for long seconds. "I do not understand this?" he finally said.

"Understand what?"

"Just why are you here, señor?"

"That's a hell of a question," Val snapped. "Why else would I be here?"

"You mean you thought you might be able to save them from the savages? Alone?"

"I had to make a try at it, at least, didn't I?"

"I have trouble believing this," Pedro said slowly.

"Believe what you blasted well want to believe. They've got a girl and a child. What else did you think a man would do, turn tail and run?"

"Many would," the Yaqui said dryly. He continued to study Val for seconds. Suddenly he came to a decision.

"I will bring up my horse and pack animal." He pointed ahead. "There is a *barranca* a short ride in that direction. I sighted it from a ridge. I will join you there. It will give us cover. Wait for me there."

It was Val's turn to study the Yaqui. "You mean we're in this together?"

"That depends, señor."

"On what?"

Pedro Jaguar did not answer that. Val understood. The Yaqui was not convinced that Val would go through with this. He expected Val to demand some sort of a deal in return for taking the risk. He was presenting a stony front, determined to offer no concessions in the matter of the murder charge.

"To hell with you!" Val snapped. "I'm asking no favors. Fetch up your animals. But why go in that direction? What about the other two bunches?"

"That one is the right one. It is the one to follow."

"How do you know?"

Pedro became angry and forgot his precise diction. "Because I see weeth my eyes. Ees eet that you are blind after all the theengs I have tell you? Do you not see that eet ees thees horse they ride, the señorita and the *niña?*"

He was pointing impatiently at the hoofmarks of a shod horse among the medley of prints on soft underfooting. There were at least four other shod animals which had passed that way among the stock that had been driven off by the Sioux. Val started to point out that fact.

"Bah!" Pedro interrupted him. "Eet ees blind you are. Do you not see that thees ees the only one carrying weight? Eet ees the sorrel gelding from Shorty Long's string. How do I know? I shod thees horse myself down the trail. I know my own work. Shorty, he kept it under saddle at night and eet was his morning horse, too. The savages, they took it. They forced the señorita to ride it because it was saddled."

He added, "The *niña,* she is weeth her."

"Now how do you know that?"

Pedro gave him a disparaging glare. "I know eet."

"You *can't* be sure both Sheila and the child are on that horse," Val said. "I don't believe in your black magic."

"I am sure because I am sure the señorita would not be parted from the little one," Pedro said stiffly. "She is not a stick to be broken easily by these savages. I am sure they quickly learned to respect her spirit. Else they would have killed them both before this."

"You may be right," Val admitted. "If any woman could stand up to them, it'd be Sheila. We're still wasting time. Let's get going."

"There's no great hurry."

"No hurry?"

"We can do nothing until they camp for the night. We do not want to be discovered. We must stay at a distance until dark."

Pedro hurried away. Val mounted and rode to the gully Pedro had designated. After a few minutes the Yaqui joined him. Pedro was mounted on a tough cow-pony and led an equally sinewy packhorse which carried a tarp-covered camp outfit.

Pedro eyed the big black horse, pleased. "You made a good choice when you stole Señor Zack's mount," he said. "He was very angry when he found that it was Comanche you had taken. I say now it was a fine thing. A good *caballo* is very nice to have when one travels as we do."

"I'll need a little more than my bare hands

if we bump into these Indians," Val said. "How about it?"

Pedro gave a snort of feigned disdain and handed back his rifle and six-shooter. "See that you use thees weapons on the right persons," he said. "I warn you I have eyes in the back of my head."

"Use the pair that are in front of your thick skull, Yaqui," Val said. "They're the ones you need — the only ones."

Pedro swung his horse around and headed along the twisting course of the gully. The segment of the raiding party had preferred the open flats above rather than the harder going in the streambed, but Pedro dismounted and made sure on foot that they were paralleling the course of their quarry.

"There is water far ahead," Pedro finally said on one of his returns from scouting the open flats. "I sighted trees and brush. That is where they will camp for the night. It is perhaps that they are already camped."

"Have you got a plan when we move up on them?" Val asked.

"It is in God's hands."

"Indians don't want to be caught with white women as captives," Val said. "I don't think either of them will be alive another twenty-four hours. It'll have to be night, or not at all."

"That is true. It is also true that we may have help from the demons as well as from God."

"More black magic?"

"They do not expect pursuit so soon. They have not been traveling fast. They will build a big fire and count coup tonight. They will strut, and dance and boast of their great bravery and their strength in shooting down those poor *vaqueros*. Those were *amigos*, señor. My friends. It grieved me to see the manner in which they were treated after they were slain. It made me angry. It made me want to avenge them."

Val nodded in agreement.

"One reason the señorita is still alive is that the savages will want to force her to watch their boasting and posturing. They will taunt her, try to torture her with stories of how her *comaradas* died."

He added, "And I theenk they will get very, very drunk. That is where the demons weel help us. The demons of alcohol."

"Alcohol?"

"Whisky. In one of the wagons was a keg of very fine Kentucky whisky that Señor Zack purchased at Julesburg for his personal use. I made sure it was missing. The savages took it. They will drink it. Tonight, I

113

am sure. As I mentioned, *El Diablo*'s imps may help us."

"You know, Yaqui, I'm beginning to believe in this magic of yours. Here's to *El Diablo* and his imps. Here's hoping they drink deep."

They pushed the horses ahead. "God has seen to it that this *barranca* was here to shield us from discovery," Pedro said. "Let us pray that He also sees to it that we are not too late. When they are drunk they are worse."

Val felt the tautness all through him. He saw something of this in Pedro's seamed face. This was a duel with something far worse than death.

The storm continued to stay its hand. Pedro said in a dry husk of a voice, "It truly shows that God is on our side. He is holding back the snow with His holy hands."

The mists thickened as twilight approached, giving them cover so that they felt safe in leaving the tortuous route of the gully and follow open country. Here the wind sighed and moaned. This was a land of ghosts. Great outcrops of boulders and tilted strata rock would loom out of the grayness like monsters. At their feet the trail of the Indians was plain to even Val's eyes. Clumps of brush would rise like tall trees and great boulders would seemingly be no bigger than a man until they drew close at hand. The sound of the hoofs of the four animals seemed agonizingly loud to Val.

He had lost all sense of direction. He began to ask himself if the Yaqui was only guessing. For all he knew they might stumble upon the Indians at any moment. There was no right or left, no up or down in the deepening fog. The only reality was the faint marks of hoofs they followed.

Abruptly Pedro halted his horse, lifting an arm as a signal. "We will leave the *caballos* here," he murmured. "They did not camp on the stream as I had believed they would. They decided on shelter from the wind in the *malpais* beyond, I think."

Val discovered that he had to use his hands to lift his leg over the saddle. He slid to the ground woodenly, so numbed had he become from cold and tension. He had not realized how swiftly dusk was coming. He flailed his arms until they were of some use to him, then took the rifle from the boot and followed Pedro's example in making sure both the action of the long gun and the six-shooter were in order.

Pedro peered at him in the freezing twilight. "How far weel you go?" he asked tersely.

Val knew what he meant. It was not a

matter of yards or miles.

"To the end! And how far will you go, Yaqui?"

"If we come out of this alive," Pedro said, "you must not expect mercy. You are wanted for killing Señor Boone. He is her brother. She loved him. He was like a son to me."

Pedro paused and when he resumed there was a vast protest and dreary desolation in his voice. "You were like a son to me also — once. That is no longer so. What I am telling you is that there can be no forgiveness. You must understand that."

"I understand," Val said. "And I understand that Boone was like a brother to me too. But I don't understand that I could have killed him. Or why."

"You will be hanged," Pedro said. "*El patrón* will see to that. He took the vow on his son's grave."

"I'll take my chances. I know I'm being a fool," Val said. "I know it was Shelia who recognized me at Wagonbow and put Zack and the crew on me. They burned me out. I was to have been married. I'd worked for years to forget the past and amount to something, to have a wife and family. And peace. Peace of mind. All that went in one night because Sheila knew who I was."

"Why are you so sure it was the Señorita

116

Sheila who did this?" Pedro asked.

"It was Sheila or you. I met both of you, face-to-face on the road just outside of Wagonbow that afternoon. At the time I didn't believe either of you recognized me. I was wrong. You weren't the one, Pedro. I'm sure of that."

"I was not the one," Pedro said.

"Then it was Sheila," Val said.

"What difference does it make?" Pedro demanded.

"None at all," Val said. "Just none at all, I guess." But he had hoped it would be otherwise.

"The eyes of some women are sharp," Pedro said. "And the hearts of some are very, very hard."

There was a strange quality in Pedro's voice. It sounded almost like pity. The Yaqui said nothing more. In silence Val followed him on the trail. Darkness was falling rapidly, but Pedro seemed to have the eyes for it. Val found that they were entering between the walls of a ravine and climbing rapidly. The cleft was wide enough for the horses.

Presently he heard the sounds of Indians talking, chanting, laughing, singing, boasting. Drunken voices.

"As I had hoped, they walk hand-in-hand with *El Diablo*," Pedro murmured.

117

6

✳✳✳✳✳✳✳✳✳✳✳✳✳✳✳✳✳✳✳✳✳✳✳✳✳

They retreated until they found a small side ravine that joined the main defile. They worked their way up this until they reached the rim, along which they crept. Finally they were looking down on the Indian camp. The ravine had shallowed and broadened at this point so that they were within pistol range.

The keg had been broached. Indians were leaping and dancing around the fire, whooping and brandishing buffalo horns from which whisky sloshed. There were eight of them. They were Sioux as Pedro had surmised.

Buffalo ribs were blackening on spits over the big fire but were going uneaten in favor of the whisky. Sheila and Penny were still alive. Sheila was huddled against a boulder and had Penny in her arms. Sheila's hair straggled over her face. She clutched the child close to her and was trying to make themselves as inconspicuous as possible in the bedlam around them.

Val had picked up enough of the Sioux tongue to understand a few words of the bragging and declamations. These were young braves. One was declaring loudly that he was Hawk Claw, son of a chief and now a great warrior in his own right and that this was the start of the thousand scalps he would take before he rode to join his forefathers in the sky.

Another drunkenly gave him a scornful shove, sending him sprawling to the ground. That was an unforgivable insult in the Indian code. The felled brave tried to rise, tugging at the knife in his belt, then collapsed and lay snoring on his back.

"Young fools!" Pedro murmured. "No guards out. Their first kill. Their first scalp."

One of the Sioux, blanket dragging in the dust from his waist, began cavorting wildly in front of Sheila, whirling an ax and screeching fiendishly. The ax came within inches of Sheila's head. Penny began to scream hysterically, for she expected to be brained by their tormentor.

Indeed, the chances were that she would be any moment as the brave incited himself to greater frenzy. Val raised his rifle and drew a bead. Whisky saved the Indian from death at that moment, for he became overbalanced by his own violence, staggered backward and sat down. He failed ignominiously when he tried to get back on his feet.

"Patience!" Pedro murmured. "Let the whisky do the work for us."

But it was not to be that easy. Another brave staggered to the captives and tried to drag the child from Sheila's arms. She clung desperately. The Sioux seized her by the hair and laughed as he inflicted pain, attempting to force her to release Penny.

Again Val steadied his aim. He held his fire for there was the chance a bullet at this angle might tear through the Indian and into Sheila or the child.

"Wait!" Pedro again pleaded. "Wait!" But he had also lifted his rifle and was ready to kill.

Sheila arose suddenly to her feet, a maneuver the young Sioux did not expect. He reeled forward and fell on hands and knees. He got to his feet, staggering. His companions were roaring with laughter and pointing derisive fingers at him.

That sent him into a murderous fury. He snatched up a war ax and rushed upon the captives. Val could see the waxen faces of Sheila and her niece as they waited helplessly for death.

He pulled the trigger. He realized that Pedro had fired at the same moment. Both bullets struck their target with the force of sledges, hurling him aside. The ax flew from his hand. The breech-clad body toppled with the limpness of a rag doll to the ground at Sheila's feet.

For the space of three heartbeats there was only the clanging echoes of the gunshots reverberating from rock walls in the darkness. The fixed look on the faces of Sheila and the child did not seem to change. Little Penny's eyes were wide, unblinking as though she had gone into a trance of terror. Sheila's face held the same glaze of resignation.

The remaining Indians seemed paralyzed for seconds. The truth registered on their alcohol-numbed minds and they made a stumbling rush for weapons and for cover.

Pedro fired twice more and two more Indians were hit. Val held his fire. He arose and leaped down the slant into the camp. He knew what the next move would be on the part of the Sioux. They would think first of killing the captives, of robbing the attackers of the prize they had come for. That was the way it went in the warfare between the two races.

He ran toward the prisoners. He saw now that both Sheila and the child were bound with thongs at the ankles. Their arms had been left free.

A thrown war ax grazed his hat. He heard Pedro's rifle blast again and saw a red body floundering. Except for the dead brave who lay near the captives, and the wounded Indian whose legs kept contorting and straightening in agony the Sioux had vanished from the light of the fire.

A rifle flashed in the darkness beyond the fire. Val also heard the twang of a bowstring along with the cold sound of the arrow as it passed close by.

He pushed Sheila and the child down flat, back of a boulder against which they had been crouching. He fumbled for the knife the Blakes had given him. His cold-numbed fingers would not respond to his frenzied need for haste. A bullet kicked earth over him and an arrow glanced from the boulder with a wicked buzz.

Pedro Jaguar pushed him aside, knife in hand and slashed the bonds. "Come!" he panted, snatching up the child.

Sheila attempted to rise and toppled, her legs too numbed to respond. Val caught her, swung her into his arms and raced in Pedro's wake, heading for cover beyond the camp circle.

An arrow plucked savagely at the sheepskin collar of his coat, throwing him off stride so that he went sprawling with Sheila in his arms. He managed to twist his body so that he took the brunt of the fall. He came to his feet, carrying Sheila with him and dove to cover among brush and boulders. Pedro, nearby, emptied the last shells from his rifle, then began firing with his .44. If the Sioux had any notion of rushing them, that discouraged it.

Horses were rearing and snorting nearby. Val saw that they were held in a rawhide rope corral. He managed to get out his knife and slashed the rope, letting the animals stream down the ravine into the darkness.

He returned and picked up Sheila again. She said faintly, "Penny? Where's Penny?"

"Here, *mia querido*," Pedro wheezed. "Are you hurt?"

"I don't know," Sheila replied in a faint voice.

The Indians still failed to charge them. No doubt they had sobered considerably, but were still befuddled. In addition they had lost some of their number and had no way of knowing but that there might be other foes around.

Val and Pedro retreated again, carrying their burdens. The light of the Indian campfire faded back of them. They finally made their way out of the defile and across the flat to where they had left their horses. Once more it was the Yaqui who led the way to the animals with uncanny sense of direction in the icy fog.

"You can put me down," Sheila said. Her voice was stronger. "I'm all right. I'm not hurt."

Val placed her on her feet and steadied her until she was walking surely. Her thoughts were for her niece. She took Penny from Pedro's arms and mothered her. "Everything's all right now, darling," she said. "Pedro's here. Pedro Jaguar. He came to take us home. The Indians are gone."

Penny had been too terrified to make a sound. Now she began to sob and cling tightly to Sheila who kept soothing her and assuring her she was safe.

This was far from the truth, of course. They were probably safe for the moment at least. Val doubted that the Sioux would make any serious attempt to find them at night. But there was another factor that was in his mind and he assumed Pedro had thought of it also.

Everything pointed to the probability that there were other Sioux near. A big village, perhaps. The buffalo meat the braves had been cooking indicated that this had been their base camp, from which they had gone out scouting and had come upon bigger game on the trail and had taken advantage of the chance to ambush what they considered invaders of their domain.

If these young Sioux had been merely a hunting party, it meant that they would soon be on their way to contact their tribesmen with word that the bigger game was still around. The fact that a white woman was among the quarry would spur the pursuit.

There would also be the deaths of the young braves to avenge. Any of them, man or woman, who fell into the hands of the Sioux now would pay a high price.

"We'll shift what grub we can to the mule," Val said. "Will that packhorse of yours let Sheila and the child ride him?"

"I theenk so, surely," Pedro said. "He is a gentle horse." Pedro seemed short of breath. He was leaning against a boulder.

Sheila moved close to Val, still holding Penny in her arms. She tried to peer in the darkness. "Who are you?" she demanded. "Do I know you?"

Val did not answer. He freed the pack from the mule and began preparing to add to its contents from what they needed of Pedro's supplies. He found the stockings and shoes he had brought from the wagon, along with other feminine garments and handed them to her. Sheila and Penny evidently had managed to clothe themselves partly before the Sioux had dragged them from the wagon, but their feet had only been protected by cloths that Sheila had managed to wrap them in.

"Here's your clothes," Val said. "I fetched them from the wagon."

Sheila busied herself clothing Penny more adequately, then herself. She kept trying to peer at Val. "I asked you who you were?" she spoke again. There was a rising pitch to her voice. Val realized she already had guessed the truth.

"I go by the name of Dave Land," he snapped gruffly.

"Or by your real name which is Val Lang!" she almost screamed.

Pedro spoke, still short-breathed. "Tomorrow will be time enough for that. We must ride. And pray for snow."

"Not with him!" Sheila choked. "Not with *him!*"

"Suit yourself," Val exploded. "Ride with me or stay here until the Sioux find you. I didn't ask for this. Why couldn't you Irons have stayed out of my life? Why follow me? Why burn me out, ruin me?"

"You know why!" She was weeping wildly. "Pedro, why don't you shoot him? You said you would. My father gave orders that he was to be shot if they couldn't bring him in alive."

Pedro did not answer. He wasn't leaning against the boulder any longer. He was slumping against it.

Val leaped to his side. "What's wrong?"

Pedro began to slide to the ground. Val caught him and supported him. His hand touched something alien that jutted from Pedro's back. A Sioux arrow.

He lowered Pedro face down on the ground and explored with his fingers in the darkness. The arrow seemed to have entered the Yaqui's back below the right shoulder blade. He fumbled for his matches, taking a chance that a Sioux might be waiting for such a target, ignited one, cupped it from the wind long enough to get a dim but better look at the situation.

Saliva was bubbling around Pedro's lips as he breathed hard in agony, but there was no stain of crimson. That gave hope that the arrow had not found his lung. It was not feasible to remove the head of the arrow under the circumstances. Val broke off the shaft, leaving a short stub jutting from the Yaqui's back.

Sheila had been close at his side and was now waiting to hear his decision. "Are you in shape to give me a hand?" he asked.

"We'll have to lift him across the packhorse. You and Penny will take his horse."

"Is — is it bad?"

"Yes."

"Won't it make it worse, lying across a horse?"

Pedro had revived enough to know what they were saying. "It must be done, señorita," he mumbled. "We cannot stay here. We will all die. We must run. Hide. There will be more of them after us to-morrow. Many more. Do as he says."

She offered no more objections. Pedro insisted that he would be able to sit in the saddle on his horse, but he was wrong. He fainted when he tried to mount. Val, with Sheila's help, placed him across a pad of blankets on the packhorse and threw a hitch around him to hold him on. He paused often in the task to make sure Pedro was still alive.

The Yaqui continued to breath haltingly, but he was in a coma and Val doubted that he would last much longer. He considered going against his better judgment and making a stand where they were.

The Yaqui seemed to sense that through his pain, and spoke out. "Go on, go on! I would rather die this way than see the *niña* and the señorita fall into their hands. I would rather die now than fall into their hands myself."

Val lifted Sheila onto Pedro's horse before she could protest, then placed Penny in her arms. He tied the lead rope of the heavily laden mule to the saddle of Sheila's mount and led the packhorse that carried Pedro. They moved through the bitter chill of the icy fog.

Val had little idea of direction. He was remembering the ghostly outcrop of boulders in the area they had passed through during the afternoon. At the time he had marked it as offering a dozen places where fugitives could hide and from which they would make a stand in case of necessity.

Finding his way back to it in this blankness was another matter. Then, once more he felt the icy touch of snow in his face. Pedro's prayers had been answered. The storm had finally arrived. Just as it had erased his trail in Val's flight from the *Sí-Sí* men after the burning of the tall house it would give them an additional margin of time in the game of life and death against the Sioux. It was not an unmixed blessing, however. It added to their physical misery and unless they found shelter it could mean the death of them all.

The snow was driven by a wind that cut to

the bone. The temperature was plunging. Val got blankets from the pack and wrapped Pedro in them. He also draped them around the shoulders of Sheila and Penny and covered them with a tarp.

"I don't want to accept favors from you, Val Lang," Sheila managed to say in an exhausted voice.

Val said nothing. He let the big black horse find its own way, depending on it to backtrack. The snow whitened the country, giving faint luminosity that enabled him to mark out the brush and to avoid treacherous gullies.

He began pausing at shorter intervals to dismount and inspect Pedro. The Yaqui, amazingly, not only clung to life but seemed stronger. He was able to talk at times.

"Camp soon," Pedro managed to articulate. "Do not wait until daylight. The snow may stop. Then your trail will be easy for them to find in new snow. Stop and hide and give the snow a chance to cover our tracks."

But it was impossible to find a hiding place in the storm. Val was forced to let the animals plod ahead. The black horse bore on into the storm willingly, as though it was never in doubt as to their destination.

The horse's instinct was right. Val realized that the animal backtrailed until he recognized the very place he had in mind — the great valley where enormous strands of boulders and tilted strata of sandstone and slate began to loom on every hand through the driving snow.

He began peering at these monsters that inhabited this valley of the giants, pausing to dismount and flounder around the bases of some, seeking some sort of a feasible path into their hearts which the horses could mount.

Sheila helped, leaving Penny on the horse, and fighting her way through the snow-covered boulders to seek refuge. It was she who found the one that served their purpose. She called to Val and he came hurrying to her side.

A slit wide enough for horses offered a possible path upward into one of these gigantic outcrops that were miniature badlands in themselves. Val ascended through the slit in the darkness. He fought his way a hundred feet or more above the valley floor and the slit widened into a long flat sheet of rock with overhanging boulders on the left that offered shelter from the weather.

"The Lord is still with us," he told Sheila as he came sliding and leaping back. "We've got a possible hideout. I'm not sure that the horses can make it, but we've got to try."

The horses made it. It was as though they realized it was now or never and they scrambled over icy boulders, aided by Val and Sheila who tugged at the reins. Finally they reached the narrow defile and Val said, "This is it."

There was no other choice. He was about played out. He knew that Sheila was worse off, as well as Penny. They had died a hundred deaths since the raid on the *Si-Si* wagons. Sheila still carried Penny in her arms. The child had been claimed at last by complete exhaustion, and while she moaned in her dreams she clung to her aunt as though knowing this was her haven of final safety.

Val removed the pack, opened it under the shelter of the overhang and spread a tarp and blankets upon which he laid Pedro Jaguar. He was able to find dried twigs and windblown grass in the crevices with which he got a fire going.

"I'll have to take care of the horses," he told Sheila.

He found another alcove not far above the one in which he had started their camp that promised to offer shelter for the animals, and he led them there, loosening cinches and tethering them as best he could in the darkness.

By the time he returned to camp Sheila had fanned the fire to warming life and was bending over Pedro. He rubbed his cold-stiff hands over the flame and finally spoke to Pedro whose eyes were open. "I'll take a look at that scratch now, *amigo*. I'll borrow your hiding knife. It looks like it can do the job better than mine."

"In my pack you will find a leather case that contains things even better," Pedro said, forcing each word with an effort. "Probes and a surgeon's scalpel. Also a few vials of chloroform. I would appreciate use of the chloroform. I am an old man. Once the Kiowas caught me and tortured me and I laughed at them until the *vaqueros* came and killed them. I fear I cannot laugh at pain now. I am ashamed."

"You should be ashamed only of pretending to be an old man," Val said. "You only want an excuse to act like a baby."

He remembered Pedro's medical kit. The old Yaqui had been doctor and surgeon for the *Si-Si* crew, rendering first aid for injuries, and administering potions from herbs and roots that he brewed. Val had seen him set and splint broken bones in roundup camps. Pedro had also taken care of more than one bullet wound in his time. He had also removed arrowheads from flesh. He knew what he was facing.

"I will enjoy seeing you squirm," Val said.

"Ha!" Pedro groaned. "I will not give you that enjoyment, señor. Do not bother with the chloroform. I had forgotten that I was a Yaqui, son of a chief."

It was Sheila who found the medical kit. She slit Pedro's coat and shirt away to expose the wound. The head of the arrow was buried deeper than Val had hoped.

She drew a vial of chloroform from the kit and looked at Val. He nodded. "How?" she murmured.

"I'm not sure," he said. "Try a few drops on a cloth and hold it over his mouth. Only until he passes out. Then only when he acts like he's coming out of it."

She complied. Val waited until Pedro's eyes began to roll. Then, swiftly, he drew out the arrowhead, working it from the flesh as gently as he could. Pedro gave a great moan and there was no more need for the drug. He was unconscious, perhaps dying.

Working together Val and Sheila stemmed the flow of blood. The medical kit contained material for stitching wounds. Sheila performed this task. Her skin was as colorless in the firelight as Pedro's but her fingers remained grimly steady as she plied the needle. They bound the wound and she sank back, covering her face with her hands, sobbing.

Pedro lay limp and Val feared that he was gone. Then he moaned, ever so faintly. Val sat, propping himself on his hands, his long legs stretched. He was too completely spent to attempt to rise to his feet for minutes. Sheila continued to be torn by dry sobs. It was Penny who was her strength and comfort now. The child came and clasped her aunt in her arms. "It's all right, Aunt Sheila," she said.

Val, after a time, got shakily to his feet. He added fuel to the fire. The snow was deepening beyond their shelter. The wind came in gusts, flakes hissing in the flames. He built the fire higher. The boulders reflected the warmth and helped repel the snow.

He spread the remaining tarp, and placed blankets on it. "You two will sleep now," he said to Sheila and the child. "There's no danger tonight. I'll look after Pedro if there's need."

Sheila bent over the Yaqui. "He's still making it," she said huskily. "He's still with us."

She arose and stood gazing at Val for a moment. In her face was conflict and puzzlement. Many questions seemed to be surging in her. But she decided against asking them. She said, "As you say."

She and the child curled up beneath the blanket within reach of the fire's warmth and exhaustion claimed them.

7

****

Val slept also, but awakened often to move to Pedro's side. The Yaqui continued to cling to life. He was still hanging on when daybreak came.

The snow had ended, but it lay more than half a foot deep and Val felt that it surely must have covered all traces of their arrival in their hideout. A bitter wind was worrying the powdery cover on the flats, drifting it against windward boulders and howling among the jagged rims above them. A lowering sky seemed close enough to touch. That sort of sky was an ally, however. Smoke from their fire would vanish into that background. And they needed warmth now above all, especially Pedro Jaguar. Val searched their rocky redoubt where small trees and bushes had found roothold and brought in an ample supply of fuel.

Pedro still lay in a stupor, his swarthy face bearing a grayish cast. Sheila placed a hand on his forehead, then sought the story of his pulsebeat. She looked up at Val. "I don't know," she said. "I just don't know. But he's still alive."

Val got out the floursack and the slab of bacon, along with the coffee pot and skillet. Sheila melted snow and mixed a batter of dough in the top of the floursack.

Val climbed to a higher point. Beneath the overcast the flats were a monotony of dull white, with snow whirlies spinning drearily here and there. Other stands of boulders, much like their own, bulged from the surface and crouched like waiting monsters beneath their coatings of snow.

He focused attention rigidly on objects that were moving to the north. He finally relaxed. They were elk foraging along the brushline of a stream. That was the only sign of life. The snow and the cold were their protection on this cheerless morning.

Sheila had a meal ready when he returned. Pedro's pack had yielded additional tableware, and they ate, balancing the tin plates as best they could. Penny could down only a few bites, obviously accomplishing that only to please Sheila. The child's cheeks were thin, her eyes big and feverishly bright.

On an impulse Val moved closer and stroked Penny's hair. "Everything will come out all right," he said.

Sheila made an instinctive move to draw the child away from him, but Penny brightened a little under his touch and some of the terror faded out of her small face. She even smiled a little.

"What did you see up there?" Sheila asked.

"A lot of country, a lot of snow. A dozen other ricks of rocks like this. Maybe dozens. Very rough country. A herd of elk along a stream to the north. I'd say three, four miles. Maybe five. That was all. At least with elk that close we won't starve."

"How about our horses and the mule? They'll have to eat, too."

"They'll make out. The wind is bound to broom a lot of snow into drifts so that they can get at the grass. I'll take them down this afternoon if the sign is right."

"That will leave tracks."

"It's a chance we have to take. We've got to keep the stock in some kind of shape. They're our only real hope of making it out of here. I'll do my best, of course, to keep to bare ground, but that's likely to be impossible. But they'd have to come this way and stumble right onto the tracks."

She glanced toward Pedro Jaguar. "I believe he is going to pull through. His pulse is stronger. He has the will to live and he is tough. But, even if he does make it, he won't be able to travel for some time. Days. Maybe weeks."

"That's right," Val said.

"They must know that one of us was wounded. The Indian who drew the bow probably saw the arrow strike. At least there must have been blood for them to find. They'll guess that if any of us are wounded we'll have to hide. They'll be looking for us."

"Yes," Val said.

She eyed him. "You don't seem particularly concerned. Or didn't you understand?"

"I understood. In fact I'm way ahead of you. I had all that figured out hours ago."

"I see," she said.

It was his turn to peer inquiringly at her. "Just what *do* you see?"

"I'm in no position to blame you, of course," she said evenly. "Nor to attempt to stop you, although I warn you that nothing has changed."

"Now I began to savvy," he said. "You think I'm aiming on clearing out."

"Of course. What else? I'd do the same if I were in your position, I suppose."

"But you're not in my position, are you?

Therefore you have to stay here and hang and rattle."

Penny, who had been listening, began to weep. "Please don't go away and leave us, mister," she wailed. "I'm scared. Aunt Sheila's scared. Please stay with us."

Val moved to the child and chucked her under the chin. She took his hand in both her small hands and clung. "You won't go away, will you?" she pleaded.

"Who said I was going away?" Val said. "Surely not me. Now what's all this crying about? Where's your dolly? It must need looking after."

"I ain't got a dolly," Penny sobbed. "I left it in the wagon when the bad men took me away."

"Well, that's something that can be fixed," Val said. "What you want to do is to get busy and make yourself a new dolly. I think your aunt will help you."

"I'm glad you're staying, Mr. Man," Penny said, the tears ending.

Val walked away to look after the horses. Sheila followed him. "I want it made clear . . ." she began.

"Sure," he said. "You'll still try to have me hanged at first chance."

He saw tears in her eyes. "I'm sorry," she choked. "But that's the way it is."

"As I've said before, I'll take my chances," he replied harshly. "I'm through running, through telling myself that maybe I did kill Boone while I was drunk. I know now that it isn't so. Why, I almost couldn't bring myself to shoot at that young Sioux until I had to when he was about to brain you. The poor devil. He didn't know what he was doing. He was drunk just as I was drunk that night."

"You're only saying that you could have done it," she said. "You're only making it harder for me to believe anything else. It was a bullet from your gun, the marks of your knee in the sand."

"I know," Val said. "I know. Do you believe I'd ever forget?"

There was a space of silence. "You *could* get away, you know," she finally said. "One man on a good horse would have a chance of making it."

"So?"

"You would be a fool to stay here. A wounded man, a child, a woman. I don't understand why you risked what you did to help us. You know my father will see to it that you are hung."

"I know."

"I still don't understand. Nothing you can do will make up for Boone. You are either a fool, or you are trying to be a hero, trying to prove something to yourself."

"You're overlooking something," Val said. "A little thing called being a human being. One with a conscience. There might be a conceited word for it, called honor. You've already told the reason I'm here. A wounded man, a child, a woman. You think I'm going to ride away and let them fend for themselves. All I'd have for the rest of my life is to live with myself."

She stared at him as though she had never really seen him before.

She added after a pause, "Wouldn't it be safer if we found a better place to hide?"

"I doubt it. This isn't such a bad spot. We were lucky. This whole country for miles is broken and gouged, littered with places like this. Even if the Sioux were sure we had headed in this direction they've got to do a lot of birddogging, a lot of country to case for sign of us. And I doubt if they know which way we headed."

"I hope you're not saying that just to make things look better than they are," she said. But he could see that she was desperately wanting to believe him.

She had formed her hair into a plait that hung down her back. Dark circles showed under her eyes. The woolen dress she had donned from among the garments Val had salvaged at the wagon hung limply from her shoulders.

Val remembered the golden days when she could not be discouraged from riding with him and Boone on hunting trips that often carried them across the border into Mexico where they camped for days without seeing another human being while they tracked peccaries and jaguar. She had never weakened nor asked for favors on those expeditions.

Perhaps she was recalling those days also, for a little flame of color broke the gray hue of her cheeks. She turned away and returned to camp to look after Pedro and her niece.

Val stood desolate, poignantly aware of how utter was his isolation from them — from Sheila, from the Yaqui, from Penny. He believed that Sheila almost hoped he would abandon them. For that would solve the burden that was on her own conscience, even the score.

Twilight of their first day in the hideout approached. Val had remained on the ridge during the afternoon but had seen no sign of life except for an occasional glimpse of the elk who were yarded along the brushline to the north.

The wind had cleared some of the flats so

that a dark straggle of grass showed. When the mists of twilight had shortened visibility he led the horses out of the outcrop and let them rustle. Their hoofs beat down the frozen snow over a considerable area. This left a tell-tale scar, but it would only be readily detected from a higher elevation. To a rider on the flats it would merge with the general whiteness of the terrain. At least that was what he kept telling himself as he hazed the horses up the ascent to their natural corral in the rocky alcove.

Sheila had supper on the fire. She had redressed Pedro's wound. The Yaqui was conscious and was obviously resting much more comfortably.

"*Buenas noches*, señor!" he greeted Val, trying to be brisk. "So you *did* return?"

Sheila looked up quickly from her duties at the cookfires, flushing. Then she turned back to the task. Val knew he had been the subject of discussion during his absence and that Pedro had warned her not to expect to see him again.

Pedro did not speak for a time, lying with dull eyes as Val warmed his chilled hands at the fire. "*Mucho loco!*" he finally grumbled, speaking more to himself than to anyone. "Why did he not *vamose*, as I wished him to do?"

Val's matted beard was tinged with ice. He examined Pedro's surgical kit and selected a razor-sharp knife. After the evening meal had been finished he heated water. Handicapped by lack of a mirror he scraped and scissored until he was reasonably clean shaven.

Sheila and Pedro pointedly ignored the transformation. But Penny, who was rebounding in spirit, watched with great interest and approval. She clapped her hands and cried, "Why you ain't such an old man after all, Mister Man."

"Please don't say ain't, Penny," Sheila remonstrated. "It's not proper grammar."

"But he ain'— I mean isn't an old man is he?" Penny argued. "Why he ain'— isn't any older'n you, Aunt Sheila."

Sheila made a grimace. "I don't imagine I'd be taken for a raving beauty," she said wryly. "But Mr. Man still has a few years advantage on me."

"What's advantage mean?" Penny demanded.

"It means I'm not as old as you seem to think I am," Sheila said. She laughed. It was the first time she had laughed.

"Pedro tells me that the colonel at Fort Miles told Zack Roper it was safe to travel the Deadwood now that the Indians had smoked the pipe and gone back to reservation," Val said.

"It seems that the colonel was mistaken," she said.

"Strange," Val said. "If a treaty was being signed, the colonel must have kept it secret. I hadn't heard about it. News like that would have been passed around in a hurry."

"I suppose we should have waited and made sure," she said. "But we were anxious to get to Fort Steele before winter really set in."

The flats remained vacant the next day, except for the occasional glimpse of the elk which continued to forage to the north. Sheila climbed to the lookout to spell him for a time. He remained with her for a few minutes.

"Pedro?" he asked.

"I'm not sure," she said dubiously. "He hasn't done too well since that first rebound. He can't down the salt pork or jerky. Nor the biscuits. He's terribly weak. He lost a lot of blood and isn't gaining much, if at all."

"He needs fresh meat," Val said. "We all could use some. I'll try to knock over an elk at daybreak tomorrow."

"But they might see you," she said quickly. *They* were the Sioux.

"There's no sign of any. To play it safe I'll

go out after dark, cross the flats and bush up near where I can get an easy shot when it gets light."

She shivered a little. "Tonight? You mean to stay out there all night?"

"It's the best way. The safest. Anybody crossing open ground in daytime might be spotted for miles by any Sioux who was watching from a high point."

"You'll freeze. It's turning colder. It must be almost down to zero right now."

"I'll make out. It has to be done, sooner or later. We'll be out of everything but flour in a few days. Pedro needs meat broth. Maybe a taste of elk steak too will help."

She turned, peering off to the west. It was in that direction, miles away that lay the Deadwood Trail and the looted *Si-Si* wagons. "I've been hoping the wagons had been found by this time and that the cavalry might show up, trailing the Sioux," she said.

"There's always the chance of course, but I wouldn't count on it, at least so soon," Val said. "The weather, for one thing, probably kept travel off the trail."

"Zack and the boys should have found the wagons by this time, regardless of weather," she said. "In fact, they were supposed to have caught up with us a day or so before the Sioux hit us."

"Maybe they have found them, but are looking in the wrong direction," Val said. "After all, it snowed, you know. As for the cavalry, I doubt that there'd be much more than a pretense at pursuit. After word got to them and they got a detachment out, nearly a week would be gone. In any event it would be a small affair to them and they wouldn't want to bump into a hornet's nest, like Custer did."

"It might be a small affair to the army, but not to us," Sheila said. "Nor to men like Shorty Long and Miguel and the others. Only loyalty to my father kept them in the crew. Clem and Ishmael had never wanted to leave New Mexico. They had been born as slaves. They drifted to New Mexico five or six years ago, trying to find a better way of life. Father gave them work on the *Si-Si* and decent homes in which to raise families. Their wives had gone ahead to Fort Steele with the first herds, along with their children. Now they are dead and their children have no fathers."

"You act like you're blaming yourself," Val said.

"I should never have gone ahead with the wagons when Zack and the boys didn't show up after the first day. I should have insisted on staying camped, within reach of Fort Miles.

But they'd told us there'd be no trouble."

"What happened? Why didn't Zack show up with the men?"

"I don't know. I suppose he was so worked up about catching you he kept at it. He was sure you were hiding somewhere around Wagonbow and that you'd eventually try to head south toward the railroad. He's a strongwilled man."

"Bullheaded is the right word," Val said. "But every man makes mistakes. Even Zack, though he'd never admit it. Pedro must have figured he was making one. Pedro quit him."

"Pedro tells me he'd been told by a little bird that something had happened to me and Penny. He puts a lot of faith in signs and omens. The crystal ball, or whatever he depends on, was right that time."

She added, "Zack shouldn't have burned your new house. That was another mistake. It wasn't necessary."

"You knew it was my house that burned that night?"

"Of course. I saw it when I rode past with Penny on my way to the wagon camp at Sage Creek. Never having seen a house like that outside of Santa Fe or New Orleans in my whole life I stopped a freighter and inquired about it. He told me it was built by a man named Dave Land who was making quite a reputation for himself as a cattle dealer."

Again she paused as though debating whether to continue. "He also told me you were building it for yourself and the bride you were going to marry," she added.

"I'll have to ask another favor of you," he said. "Let's just let it ride that way. Don't bring it up again."

He left her to carry on the vigil alone and returned to the camp. At midafternoon he took over the task again, staying on the windswept vantage point until dusk.

He ate the meal Sheila served, then inspected his weapons, buckling the six-shooter outside his saddlecoat. He pocketed two leftover biscuits and a few strings of leather-like jerky that remained from the supply the Blakes had furnished.

"If it figures that way, I might not chance coming back across the open stretches in daylight," he said. "Don't expect me until dark tomorrow, or later."

Penny ran to him, sobbing. "You will come back, won't you, Mr. Man?" she implored.

"Of course," he said. Sheila and Pedro said nothing. But their stony expressions were eloquent. Once more they were doubting that he would return. *"Adios!"* he said.

He saddled the black horse, led it down the treacherous descent from the hideout, mounted and rode away into the darkness. He had mapped the landmarks in his mind and set his course by them.

A flat-topped butte, which he judged was less than a mile from where he had sighted the band of elk, was his destination. There he planned to leave the horse and make the rest of the way on foot. He had not mentioned the possibility that a rifleshot might be heard by any Indians who happened to be within reach, but he knew Sheila and Pedro were aware of that hazard.

If he was successful in stalking his quarry, it was a chance that must be taken. In any event, he must make sure that a single bullet counted. Additional firing would only add to the chance of bringing trouble. Even a Sioux's ears might not be keen enough to identify the direction from which the report of a gun came unexpectedly, especially if the distance was long. That was why he had chosen to go through the ordeal of a night-long stalk of his prey in the hope he could be so close when daylight came he could not miss.

The flat butte arose ahead of him, drew nearer with agonizing slowness, then finally stood black and huge before him. He found cover for the horse among scattered big boulders and left it hobbled and picketed where it would stay interested in prospecting for the scant forage.

He had guessed that the butte was about a mile from the brush line of the stream, but discovered that he had overestimated, for he found the fringe of the brush looming ahead before he had expected it. He halted instantly, freezing, berating himself, fearing he might already have alarmed his quarry.

But no sound came. He also became aware that the wind had lost its razor bite, and was turning raw and damp. Once again the changeable weather was bringing the threat of a rain and thaw. At this moment rain was the last thing he would appreciate.

He advanced a step at a time now, testing each foothold before placing his weight on it. Once the snow squeaked beneath his feet and he stood for a long, breathless minute or two, fearing the result.

Still silence. He began to believe he was on a wild goose hunt. The quarry might have moved elsewhere. He crept ahead again with infinite caution. It was muscle-taut, nerve-strung action in slow motion that took as much out of a man as violent exertion.

Then he froze. The wind had shifted slightly, bringing sound, faint at first, then very definite. He edged ahead even more slowly. He could hear animals breathing and snuffling, and heavy hoofs moving sluggishly. Brush rose thickly around him. The elk evidently were yarded just ahead.

He crept to a hollow which offered concealment and settled down to wait out the night. It was a harsh vigil where time seemed to stand still. The snow began to thaw, adding to his misery. He was forced to his feet or risk being soaked to the skin as icy water began to form around him.

This added to the danger that he might be discovered by the elk. The animals were moving around in the darkness, made restless by the change of weather. The wind was in his favor, but if it shifted they probably would catch his scent and stampede.

He was nearer his quarry than he wanted to be. He could only stand motionless, waiting. After a time the elk seemed to have drifted to a safer distance and were settling down.

When the first wan promise of dawn came in the sky he tried to tell himself it was only imagination again, for he had built up false hope several times during the long ordeal. This time it was real daybreak.

Clouds had moved in. It began to rain, a cold wintry downpour. It was almost the last straw. He was chilled to the marrow, utterly desolate of spirit.

He became aware that the last mists of night were gone. A cow elk and a young bull that appeared to be a yearling stood less than a hundred yards away. An easy kill.

He had shielded the rifle beneath the skirt of his coat. Inch by inch he freed the gun and raised it, nestled against his shoulder and looked over the sights. He kept counseling himself to take it slow, to make sure. He wanted the yearling. The cow appeared old, and it was big and would be difficult to handle with only a skinning knife. Even the yearling would offer enough of a problem when it came to skinning and taking meat.

He wanted no siege of buck fever now. He had made far more difficult shots than this scores of times without a tremor, steady of hand, absolutely sure of his target. There had been little at stake on these occasions. Now everything was at stake.

He flexed his trigger finger before letting it approach the weapon. The quarry was a few strides nearer, if anything, completely unsuspicious. He braced himself for this easy kill, his finger beginning to squeeze the trigger.

He paused. Both the cow and the young elk seemed to move violently. In his ears were the sounds of gunshots. But not from his rifle. He had not fired. Stunned, he watched the elk turn to run. The cow took two strides, then crumpled. Another brace of shots sounded and the yearling went down.

Yells and grunts of satisfaction arose. Four blanket-draped Sioux burst from cover well to Val's right and came running to their kills. They were young braves, jubilant over the easy hunt.

Val sank flat in the brush. They had been too intent on the game to have discovered that another hunter was present. He huddled there, the rifle ready in case they sighted him. From the sounds he knew they were gutting their kills. Then came the skinning. He could hear the sound of axes as bone joints were severed. Guttural talk, laughter, horseplay and obviously joshing and boasting.

It went on for more than an hour, though it seemed an agony of time to him. Finally he heard them bringing up the ponies and loading the meat. After a time the sound of their voices and the slogging of unshod hoofs in the slushy snow faded off downstream. He chanced a glance and glimpsed four Indians riding away, leading two packponies that carried jostling loads slung

156

in the fresh hides of the two elk.

Val waited a long time. It might be a trap. They might have sighted him and were baiting him into making an easy target of himself rather than try to run him down. More of them might be bushed up, guns and arrows ready.

Time passed. He could stand it no longer. The depression in which he lay was turning into a lake of cold water. Even though he knew how patient an Indian could be in awaiting a kill, particularly a kill such as this, he had to take the chance, force the issue if they were still around.

He left his hideout and crawled through the wet snow on hands and knees. He came at last in sight of the remains of the two elk. Two gray wolves had already arrived and were beginning to worry the carcasses. Ravens circled overhead, sounding a raucous call that was sure to bring more of their kind. Half a dozen coyote hovered at a distance, waiting for their turn after the formidable wolves had sated themselves.

The beasts of the plains would not have moved in so boldly if Indians had been around. Val arose and ran into the clearing. The two wolves retreated reluctantly, sounding growls of protest. One whirled and charged him, and he was forced to fire and kill or be taken by the throat. The mate of the downed animal backed off, standing yellow-eyed but deciding not to attack.

Val hoped that enough time had elapsed so that the Sioux hunters would be out of hearing of the shot. He moved in and examined what they had left of the elk. Evidently game was plentiful, for they had taken only the choicest parts of the quarters and the saddle, in addition to the hides. He remembered the buffalo meat that had been in the base camp of the young Sioux who had held Sheila and the child captive. He surmised that the elk had been slain more for their hides than the meat.

But what meat was left might mean the difference between starvation or survival for himself and the others. He worked fast with the skinning knife and soon had all the meat he could carry slung over his shoulder in the tarp he had brought. As he moved away, the coyotes and the wolf crept in. So did a cloud of ravens. He could hear the snarling and the squawking as he headed away.

He returned to where he had left the black horse. Rain was drenching the flats, erasing the snow, but visibility under the clouds was good. There were undoubtedly other Indians near and he decided against trying to cross the open flats in daylight. He tried to find shelter, but the best he could do was to huddle among brush where at least he was hidden from sight, and tough it out. The horse was equally miserable, fighting the hobble and tether until it finally became sadly resigned to the chill rain.

When twilight came he lashed the pack on the horse, mounted and rode for the hideout. Total darkness fell swiftly, but the black horse seemed to feel that it was homeward bound and carried him unerringly to the narrow slit that ascended to their camp.

He saw the warm glint of firelight before he reached the alcove, and smelled the fragrance of coffee being boiled. He dismounted, swung down the cargo of elk meat and said, "This ought to stick to your ribs, Yaqui."

He had been blinded a little by the firelight. A figure was standing in front of him. He found himself looking into the bore of a six-shooter. Above the cocked hammer of the gun was the big, unshaven face of Zack Roper!

"Put up your hands, Val, high and straight," Zack said. "I'd be happy to put a slug in you if you move."

Val lifted his arms. In the background Sheila stood with Penny at her side. Sheila's lips were stiff-set and ashen. Penny was sobbing. Pedro Jaguar had lifted his head from his blanket pallet and was watching, his weathered face as devoid of expression as a brown stone.

8

****

"Turn around," Zack commanded. When Val obeyed the big man moved in and took his six-shooter and the skinning knife. He then removed the rifle from the saddle of the black horse.

He shoved Val into a position where he stepped into the loop of a rope placed on the ground. He jerked the loop taut, snaring Val's ankles. He then dropped the loop of a second picketline over Val's shoulders, pinning his arms at his sides.

Val looked at Sheila. "I hardly expected such a welcome home," he said.

She would not look at him. "Where did you drop in from, Zack?" he asked.

"I'm here," Zack said. He was bulkier than ever in his winter garb, over which he wore a black slicker that came to his boottops. His rainsoggy hat stood near the fire, drying. His thick, dark hair was long and wiry, as was his growth of black whiskers. Val noted that Zack was beginning to be touched by a tinge of frost around the temples, although he could hardly be more than in his middle thirties. His eyes were bloodshot from weariness beneath heavy brows.

Val saw that a mud-spattered horse and a packhorse bearing the *Si-Si* brand had been added to their hold of stock.

"At least you didn't fly here, Zack," he said. "You came on a horse, just like a human being. Where are the others — the *Si-Si* riders?"

"What's it to you?" Zack said.

"If they're out there still looking for me, they might have bad luck," Val said. "There are people in these parts who like to tie cowboys to stakes and set fire to them. Some of those boys might be old friends of mine, like Shorty Long and Miguel were."

"You've got no friends," Zack said. "But, if it really weighs on your mind you can quit worrying about them. They're probably back in Wagonbow by this time."

"Wagonbow?"

"I sent a couple of them hightailing it back to build a fire under the cavalry," Zack said. "I sent the rest of them back with the wagons."

"You sent everybody back?" Val said, puzzled. "What about you?"

"I figured one man would have a better chance of finding out what had become of Sheila and the young one than if a whole crowd of us went slamming across country. Pedro had left a note saying the Indians had headed in this direction. So here I am."

He inspected the contents of the pack Val had unloaded from the black horse. "Elk steaks," he said exultantly. "I've been living on beans and smoked pigbelly. Better yet, I get my horse back. Old Comanche. And he looks like he's in pretty good shape. So there's elk around here? At least we won't starve. There must be buffalo too. I spotted some wallows and some old sign. Where did you bag the elk?"

"I didn't. All I bagged was a wolf."

"How come?"

"A couple of Sioux knocked over the elk before I could pull the trigger, lucky for me. They never knew I was around. I flattened out like a pancake in the brush and waited until they'd taken the hides and what meat they wanted. I fought with the wolves and coyotes for our share of what was left. You'll find some of it a little stringy. The Sioux took the choice parts. But beggars can't be too choosy."

"Sioux? Where? How many?"

"Well they were less than five miles away

at the time, but they pulled out and headed east. There were four of them. Young braves — like the ones that hit your wagons. But I don't think they were from the same bunch. Pedro sort of did enough damage to the others so that I doubt if they felt like going on any more hunting trips for a while at least."

"Only four?" Zack snorted disdainfully. "And you let them just ride away without plowing into 'em?"

Val cocked an eyebrow at him. "Now that you mention it," he said caustically, "that's exactly what I did. It's a habit of mine, avoiding such things as rattlesnakes, buzz-saws and four-to-one odds."

"Yeah, you're better at hunkerin' back of a rock an' shootin' a drunken man in the back."

"You may be right," Val said slowly. "Then, again, you may be wrong. Anyway I feel that they were just scouting and happened to spot the elk. Squaws like elkhide to work with for moccasins and such. These four took the hides. If they were a long way from home, they probably wouldn't have bothered. So, squaws might not be too far away. That means either a village, or a big hunting party. The Sioux will be doing their best to make meat with winter coming on.

Do you follow me?"

"You seem to know a lot about these Indians," Zack said. "How come? You married to a squaw? You shore look like one of 'em. What became of the beard? Folks in Wagonbow told me you had one."

"I imagine they told you a lot of things," Val said. "And one wasn't that I was married to a squaw."

Zack laughed. He turned and spoke to Sheila. "If them Sioux was five miles away an' gittin' farther when Lang last saw 'em there's no worry. How 'bout gettin' some o' this elk provender on the fire. I'm so hungry my backbone's touchin' my belt buckle."

Sheila cooked elk steaks and made a broth for Pedro. The Yaqui's face still had that grayish hue, and he was obviously merely holding his own. When the broth was ready he managed to down the spoonfuls Sheila placed in his lips.

At Sheila's insistence Zack freed Val's right arm so that he could eat the elk meat that she cut up and passed to him on a tin plate, along with a fork. The meat did wonders. Some of the apathy faded. He had not realized how long it had been since he had eaten.

The rain tapered off. Moisture still dripped from the rocks, but the clouds had lifted. The yammer of coyotes sounded far-away. Occasionally the deeper yowl of wolves could be heard.

Pedro raised his head. "There are buffalo out there," he said. Val believed that some of the pallor had faded from the Yaqui.

"How do you know?" Zack demanded.

"The wolves, the coyotes, they follow the buffalo," Pedro said. "And so do the Indians. They all live off the buffalo."

"And how do you know that," Zack repeated scornfully. "You never hunted buffalo. There never was a buffalo west of the Pecos, you old liar."

"That is true," Pedro said. "But as a young man I hunted them on the *Llano Estacado*. And the Comanches hunted me. They did not get me. But I shot many buffalo east of the Pecos."

Val needed sleep. His head drooped as he finished the food Sheila had given him. Zack prodded him roughly awake. "Don't try to play possum," the big man warned. "I better tie you up tight ag'in." And he did so.

"Exactly how did you really find us, Zack?" Val asked.

"Ask Pedro," Zack said, grinning.

Val looked at the Yaqui. But Pedro, standing on his privilege as a chief's son, chose to refuse to speak.

166

"It was easy enough," Zack said, continuing to grin. "In addition to leaving the note at the wagon telling what had happened and that he was taking the trail, he blazed the trail. A spur drag here and there on a boulder, a flat rock on top of another, a broken tree branch. A child could have followed it. And I'm not a child."

"You could have told me," Val said accusingly to Pedro. "Zack will take me to Cass Irons, or kill me. Either way I'll be executed without a trial."

Pedro would not meet his eyes. "I should have left you lying back there with that arrow in you so the Sioux could have finished you," Val said bitterly.

"The day may come when I will wish you had been that merciful, *amigo*," the Yaqui said.

Amigo? Friend? The Yaqui had not used that term lately. Not in more than eight years.

A new thought came to Val's tired mind. "But that could only have led you to where we jumped the Sioux that night and got Sheila and the child away from them," he said to Zack. "Pedro was in no shape to blaze a trail after that arrow hit him. But you followed us here."

Even as he spoke he knew the answer. He

turned to gaze at Sheila. "You!" he said.

She met his eyes levelly. "Yes. I did it. Pedro wasn't unconscious all the time. He whispered to me to mark our route so that we could be found. I did so. I hung threads of my petticoat and such on brush and on boulders that night as we were traveling through the snowstorm. Today I saw Zack approaching out in the flat and signaled him to come in."

"Did it ever occur to you that other eyes might follow that infernal line of threads you set out?" Val asked grimly.

"At the time," she said, "it was a case of the devil or the deep sea."

"And I'm the devil, of course."

"I had to do it," she said, her lips gray, taut.

"Strange how things work out," he said. "Do you remember a Christmas Day when I tried to give you a doll and you hit the ceiling, telling me it was high time I opened my eyes?"

"That's all past and done," she choked.

"I did open my eyes that day. I made up my mind I'd start right then to try to amount to something so I'd have the right to ask you to marry me when you got a little older. I've tried to forget you ever since, even tried to make myself believe I could marry another girl and learn to love her. But you were always the one. And now you're the one that's likely to get me hung."

"Stop it!" she cried. "Stop it!"

Zack walked to Val and smashed a fist into his face. Val felt blood flow from a split lip. Zack braced himself for another punch, but Sheila rushed in and pushed him away.

"No!" she said. "Get away from him, Zack!" Val, amazed, saw that she had a cocked six-shooter in her hand.

Zack, equally astounded, backed hastily away. She suddenly lowered the pistol. The moment was over.

"Have you gone loco, Sheila?" Zack raged. "Fer a minute I thought you was goin' to shoot me! Why put a gun on *me?* Ain't you gettin' things twisted. This man murdered Boone, remember? Your brother. Don't tell me you've got any sympathy for *him?*"

"There's no point in torturing him," she said. "He's in no shape to try to get away. None of us can travel far, and he's had as bad a time as any of us."

"To hell with him," Zack snarled. "You're acting like an idiot."

"And you act like an Apache," she said. "At least make sure the ropes aren't too tight. He could lose his hands, his legs."

"Look, dearie, this is the man your father put a price of ten thousand dollars on. He's worth a fortune, dead or alive."

"Do you intend to claim that reward?" she asked icily.

"Why not?"

She did not answer, turning her back on him and walking away. Zack stood gazing after her, a strange, flinty took in his face. Val, startled, had the impression that Zack was considering drawing his gun and shooting her down. Then Zack shrugged a little as though amused.

Val began breathing regularly again. He decided that his imagination was playing tricks on him. However, there was something off key. Why had Sheila gone so far as to point a gun at Zack? And Pedro's attitude had also softened somewhat.

Sheila came to his side and eased the knots that Zack had yanked savagely tight. The needle numbness of lax circulation began to fade from his arms and legs, helping him descend into the exhausted sleep his body craved.

Daybreak was overhead when he awakened. He lay for a time trying to remember where he was and who he was. He had been dreaming of a day long ago. A day when he and Boone and Sheila — she at her own willful insistence — had ridden off on a fishing trip in one of the waters of a tributary to the Pecos. She had brought the ingredients for a meal. They had fried fish and gorged themselves on pickles and potato salad. Last of all was a bottle of champagne that Sheila had filched from her father's supply. Neither he nor Boone had taken to the bubbly flavor, and Sheila, considering herself very daring, had only tried a taste or two and had pronounced the wine as terrible.

It had been hot that day. They'd gone for a swim. Sheila had found a place to swim alone. They had ridden home whooping and gigging the horses around the ranch-house until Cass had come out, grinning and said, "Come in, you noisy varmints and sober up on lemonade. Sheila, did you have anything to drink? Tell me the truth because I'll know it anyway."

But she hadn't drank any of the champagne, and the "lemonade" Cass served him and Boone in frail, shallow, cut glasses was the same stuff, but very cold so that it tingled and bubbled in the throat and made a man feel like he could lift himself to the moon by his own bootstraps. He and Boone had made fools of themselves for sure that night. Sheila hadn't spoken to either of them for a week, being pointedly very aloof to Val. All he could remember was that he had told her he might ask her to marry him if she'd only been half a dozen years older.

It had been the cussed champagne talking, of course, but he'd never been able to figure out why Sheila had been so stiff-necked with him afterward. He'd apologized to her for it, and had tried to get her to join him in laughing about him talking of marriage to so young a girl, but that had only seemed to get him farther off on the wrong foot with her.

Things had never been the same after that. She'd quit trying to tag along with him and Boone. She began to stay aloof from a mere hired hand like Val. She began putting up her hair in a mature fashion and acting more like a lady than a tomboy. Boone was ambushed not long afterward. Val's world had changed.

He could not believe it when he opened his eyes and found that it was full daylight, so soundly had he slept. Sheila was frying more elk meat. She had biscuits browning in a dutch oven that had been among the utensils Zack had added to their equipment, along with more flour, bacon and canned goods.

Sheila warmed the broth she had made

the previous night and Pedro ate that and enjoyed solid meat. He smacked his lips. The elk meat had been his ticket to return to life. He was gaining fast.

Zack gorged himself on the elk meat and biscuits. He sat by the fire, drinking coffee from a tin cup. Sheila had built the fire of dry twigs which gave little smoke, as Val and Pedro had instructed her. It was dying down now and Zack arose and threw wet fuel on the flames. Black smoke began to rise.

"Douse that fire," Val said.

Zack whirled on him. "You ain't givin' the orders around here, fella."

"Somebody with a little common sense should," Val said. "If that thing keeps smoking, we might have a hundred Sioux down on us before the day's over."

Sheila hurried to smother the fire, tossing aside the wet fuel. After a moment Zack helped in the task. Penny helped also. A few more wisps of black smoke sailed up in spite of their efforts. They could only hope that they would not be sighted.

Zack was uneasy. He occupied the lookout spot until mid-afternoon, not returning to camp even for the noon meal. When he finally gave up he glared at Val. "There's no Sioux around," he growled. "That yarn about Indians killing them elk was just that, wasn't it — a yarn?"

"You know," Val said, "and I know it wasn't."

"Maybe you'd be better off if the Sioux had spotted that smoke this mornin'," Zack said. "It might be better than cashin' in at the end of a rope."

"Stop it!" Sheila cried. "Why talk about it?"

Zack subsided, grinning. He picked up his rifle and said, "I'll stand watch 'til dark."

Penny made a face as he walked out of camp to ascend to the lookout. She flirted the hem of her small skirt scornfully.

"Penny!" Sheila remonstrated. "That's not being ladylike."

"Zack's a meanie!" Penny said. "I wish he'd never have come here."

"That's no way to talk," Sheila said. "After all he came here to help."

"If he's such a nice man, why does he act so bad toward Mr. Man? Why does he want Mr. Man to be hung? What's that mean, Aunt Sheila? What's hung?"

"That's enough, Penny!"

Pedro, who had been listening, grunted, "For shame, *muchacha!* You ask questions your aunt cannot answer. It is time you were made to realize that this man shot your uncle, the Señor Boone. He is indeed

174

a very bad man at heart."

But Penny refused to give ground. "If he's so bad, then why did he help us?"

"Perhaps he hopes to put himself in a better light with *el patrón,* your grandfather, and be forgiven. That is not possible. He cannot be forgiven for what he did."

"Will you two quit talking about this!" Sheila cried.

Afterward Val spoke to Sheila when Penny was out of hearing, playing with a doll that she and Sheila had formed out of a stick of wood and scraps of cloth. It was Penny's great treasure, her constant companion.

"I was sure you hadn't recognized me that night," he said. "You had good control of yourself. It must have been a shock to you."

She was puzzled. "What are you talking about?"

"That evening on the trail out of Wagonbow. Don't tell me you don't know what I'm talking about. You passed me as I was driving a buggy with a young lady beside me as you were on your way to the *Si-Si* wagon camp."

She seemed further perplexed. "Why, I do vaguely recall passing a buggy containing two people," she said. "But I don't know what you mean. Who recognized you?"

Val eyed her. "What do you mean, 'vaguely remember'? I was the man in that buggy, of course. You knew me in spite of the beard I was wearing."

"No, no!" she exclaimed. "That's not the way it was. I was more interested in the lady. She was very good-looking. I remember her well, now that you mention it. You mean you were the man in the buggy? I didn't recognize you. Zack was the one."

"Zack? Where? When?"

"In town. He came riding into camp after dark greatly excited. He didn't want to tell me what it was all about but I wormed it out of him. I went along when he rode away with the boys to find you. I stayed back to watch over the horses."

Strangely, Val felt lighter in spirit. Sheila must have sensed that, for she said quickly, "Don't think for one minute I wouldn't have put Zack and the crew after you if it had really been me."

Val racked his memory, trying to decide where and when Zack had spotted him that day in Wagonbow. He retraced his course. He had ridden directly to Henry Erskine's bank, gone inside and had been there when Zack and the *Si-Si* wagons passed by on the street.

He had been careful to remain in the bank

after that, appearing only momentarily on the street as he had escorted Jane to the hitchlot where the buggy stood. It had been after dark when he returned and had mounted his horse and headed out of town.

It didn't seem possible, yet Zack must have seen him and recognized him somehow. He had passed the test against even Sheila's feminine eyes, but apparently Zack's perceptions were even keener.

He put the question to Zack himself during one of the big man's returns to camp from the lookout post to eat cold food. "Where were you when you spotted me in Wagonbow and knew who I was, Zack?" he asked.

Zack stopped chewing for a moment, peering as though surprised and not exactly knowing how to answer that question. "What makes you think it was me?" he asked.

"It *was* you, wasn't it?" Val demanded.

Zack began to grin slyly. "That's for me to know," he said. "We've got you, ain't we? That's all that matters."

A bitter suspicion crept into Val's mind, a thought so monstrous he refused to entertain it. He told himself Zack was only trying a bit of mental torture with his clumsy attempt at being mysterious. If Sheila hadn't been the one, then surely it had been Zack who had recognized him. Pedro had already denied it. There was the possibility one of the *Si-Si* riders who had known him in the past might have sighted him, but that seemed remote. It must have been Zack. There would be no other. Except one! He refused to let his mind move farther along that incredible line.

He quit talking. Zack tried to prod him into asking more questions, obviously ready with more taunting and evasive answers, but Val refused to be baited. Zack finally finished his food. He inspected Val's bonds, then gave him an openhanded slap on the check. The blow was unexpected, but did little real damage.

Sheila uttered a cry of protest. Zack snarled. "That's only to let him know what he's in for from your father."

He picked up his rifle and left camp to resume watch from the high boulders. Penny burst into tears. "Bad man!" she sobbed. "Bad man!"

This time Sheila did not correct her. She did not speak. Nor did Pedro. He watched Val with his old, inscrutable eyes as though waiting for something.

Val had nothing to say. Nothing seemed to add up. Why had the commander at Fort Miles been so mistaken about the situation as to have caused Sheila and her party to be exposed to the danger that had overtaken them? Zack's decision to follow Pedro's blazed trail alone, while sending all his men back to Wagonbow seemed bad judgment even though Zack's view that one man would be able to travel with less chance of discovery had some substance. Zack had also made a blunder in delaying so long in setting out to overtake Sheila and the wagons. His urge to capture Val had outweighed sound reasoning.

Pedro spoke softly. "You theenk he ees not telling the truth, *si?*"

Val was surprised. He eyed the Yaqui. "Why would he lie?"

"You only answer my question weeth another question that I cannot answer." After that neither had anything to say.

At least Val did not have to endure more physical punishment at Zack's hands. The big man made sure he was kept hobbled and helpless to escape, watching over him with a cocked six-shooter whenever he was freed for exercise, but otherwise let him severely alone. Val was certain Sheila had warned Zack against further violence.

Zack obstinately stood lookout from dawn to dark, permitting Sheila to spell him only at short intervals. He reported on each return to camp he had seen no sign of hostiles.

He continued to scoff at Val's story of the Indians killing the elk. "Sioux?" he jeered. "There's none within miles. I've sat on that blasted rock up there so long I've got blisters without seein' anything but coyotes an' prairie dogs."

"Was it coyotes that attacked the wagons and killed our *camaradas?*" Pedro demanded. "Was it prairie dogs that drove the arrow into me? You are being a fool. We cannot hide here much longer. They will discover us, sooner or later. This is their hunting ground. It is only by good fortune they have not come this way already."

"You're the fool, not me," Zack said. "I don't hanker at havin' to pack you along if you play out. We'll wait here 'til I'm sure you can make it."

Pedro subsided, grumbling. He was improving rapidly, and kept insisting that he would not be a burden to them. He urged that they set out at once and try to make the Deadwood Trail which lay somewhere west of them — at least a day's ride — and there wait until help came along.

But Zack continued to insist each day that they should linger in the hideout another day at least to make certain the Yaqui could travel. Val had no voice in the matter, but he felt that the tough old Yaqui was able to sit a horse and that Zack was being overly cautious.

He began to get the impression that the big man had something else in mind or was waiting for something to happen before making a move. Meanwhile the elk meat gave out and Zack shot two antelope that had wandered within range, taking a chance the shots would not be heard by foes. He and Sheila stood watch for hours but no trouble appeared.

Even so their fare was far from ample. Zack tried to keep Val on scant meals but Sheila overruled that, although she was far from favoring herself when dividing the food.

They had been in the hideout a week when Zack came hurrying back to camp at nightfall, excited.

"Tomorrow we eat buffalo beef again," he announced exultantly.

"Buffalo?" Sheila echoed.

"Nothin' else but. I sighted 'em at dusk quite a ways east, but driftin' this way. By mornin' they ought to be close enough for a shot."

"Where there are buffalo there might be Indians," Pedro spoke, alarmed.

"Not with these buffalo," Zack said. "There's no more'n a handful. Eight, ten. Maybe a dozen. If the Sioux had been after 'em, they'd have wiped out that few a long time ago."

"Why risk it?" Val said. "You've got enough of that antelope meat to carry us for a while."

"Look who's hornin' in?" Zack said angrily. "You got no hand in this, Val. Besides, I'm sick a' goat meat. I want somethin' that'll stick to my ribs."

"Such as an arrow like Pedro got?" Val said.

"I know what I'm doin'," Zack snapped. "I'll saddle up before daybreak an' be out there, holed up like you claimed you was when you dropped the elk. You didn't bring any Indians down on us, did you? I won't either, because there ain't any out there."

That was the way it was when they turned in for the night. Val slept uneasily. This Zack Roper he was seeing now was an entirely different person from the one he had known in the past. Zack had always been inclined to be headstrong and intolerant of advice, but those were often qualities necessary in a range boss who had to make decisions and stick to them, right or wrong. He had never been especially close to the riding crew, but that too was one of the penalties of being the boss. He had always seen to it that the *Si-Si* riders were well mounted, well fed and got their pay right on the dot. He knew cattle and was respected widely for his skill at organizing roundups.

Something inside Zack had deteriorated, turned dark and ugly. Val had the chill belief that Zack meant to kill him at first opportunity, and would do so without the least compunction. Only the presence of the others was preventing it.

Zack's continued insistence that there was no danger from the Sioux puzzled Val. It did not ring true. Perhaps it was only an attempt to give little Penny peace of mind, and Sheila also, although in Sheila's case she was mature enough to realize that it was only a pretense. Pedro was well able to travel and Val agreed with him that every day they spent in the hideout only heightened the chances of their discovery.

He awakened when Zack began moving around the camp, preparing to ride out to bring down a buffalo. Instead of waiting until toward morning Zack was pulling out around midnight, Val estimated. He heard Zack trying to saddle Comanche, but the black horse would have none of him and refused the bit and saddle. Zack finally gave it up rather than risk being bucked off in the narrow alcove. He used a quirt a few times on the black, then saddled the horse on which he had arrived. He finally rode away, taking the packhorse to bring in meat. Silence came again in the camp.

Val tried to sleep, but the uneasiness persisted. Zack's midnight departure in freezing darkness seemed as erratic as many of his actions lately. There was no need for starting out at such an hour. For one thing, there was no certainty the animals would continue to drift in this direction. In addition, buffalo could be stalked in daylight with far less skill than was needed in dealing with animals of keener perceptions such as elk.

Val realized that Sheila was still awake also. The creak of saddle leather and the thump of hoofs had long since faded into the night as Zack had ridden away. From the sounds he had urged the animals into a fast trot. Pedro was awake also. None said anything but Val believed they were all asking themselves the same question. Why would a man out to stalk game, risk alarming his quarry by galloping a horse? And why risk riding at that speed in darkness over rocks and perhaps gopher holes? There was no answer.

Val finally fell asleep again. He awakened once more, completely and suddenly. Daybreak was bright in the sky, outlining the higher rims above and reaching dimly into the camp.

The silence of the night had vanished. An eerie chill tingled at the nape of his neck. Something was out there — on the flats. Something vast. Not Indians. It was bigger than anything of human origin.

Sheila and Pedro had awakened also. "What is it?" she breathed, frightened.

"Buffalo!" Val said. "Sounds like a lot of them have moved in. That handful Zack said he saw before dark must have been only the start of a big herd."

Sheila dressed, pulled on boots and a jacket and climbed to the crow's nest. She returned, shivering. "There are thousands of them," she chattered. "They're all around us."

Pedro and Val looked at each other, the same thought in their minds. As Pedro had said, where there were buffalo there were sure to be Sioux.

"What could have happened to Zack?" Sheila said. "He ought to be coming back. He surely wouldn't have any trouble getting a shot by this time."

"He isn't coming back," Val said.

"Why do you say that?" she demanded. "Why —"

Pedro spoke. "He would not have taken his blankets and much of our food, if it was but to bring down a buffalo at our doorstep, *mia querida*."

Zack's bedding was gone. The bulk of their meager store of flour, salt and coffee was also missing.

Penny had awakened. She was rubbing her eyes, her thin little face heavy with sleep. "Look at the smoke, Aunt Sheila!" she exclaimed, pointing. "I thought Mr. Man told us not to let the fire make much smoke."

A black column was rising from a point higher in their hiding place. "My God!" Val exclaimed. "The Sioux can't help seeing that!"

They stared unbelievingly at each other for a moment. Only one person could have left that signal that might mean their death. Zack!

9

✳✳✳✳✳✳✳✳✳✳✳✳✳✳✳✳✳✳✳✳✳✳✳✳

"Cut me loose!" Val snapped. "Quick! We've got to put out that fire. It's probably too late to do any good, but there's always a chance. Then we'll have to get out of here. Run for it!"

"Run for it?" Sheila repeated confusedly.

"Turn me loose, I tell you!"

She complied. Together they scrambled through the rocks and found the source of the smoke. Dry fuel had been stored in a crevice a distance from the crow's nest. It had been set afire during the night and green brush thrown on it to smolder and create long-lasting smoke. Whoever had started the fire must have been collecting the fuel for days. Only Zack, who had insisted on standing watch alone, would have had the opportunity.

They desperately attempted to smother the smoking brush. They failed. The accumulation was big, the coals too hot. They lacked the material to smother it, being able to find only scant handfuls of earth and snow in the crevices around. The smoke continued to rise stubbornly.

From this elevation Val got his first look at the buffalo herd. He had listened to old-time hunters telling of herds on the prairies between the Platte and Arkansas Rivers whose size was almost beyond belief. The herd he was looking at now might not be in that class, but the flats south of their vantage point had been invaded by a mighty army of shaggy, dark giants whose numbers extended as far as the eye could carry. More buffalo were flowing sluggishly north of them, but these advance guards were scattered and extended only a few hundred yards in that direction. However, the horizon to the east was a black mass, and they could see that eventually their position would be hemmed in.

Their sudden arrival suggested to Val that they had been stampeded and were just beginning to settle down. They were still drifting west, but the majority were now beginning to graze and their ponderous movement obviously was slowing.

He scanned the flats in the distance, but he could see no sign of danger beyond the north fringe of the herd.

"But if the Sioux are out there they've

seen the smoke," he told Sheila. "They'll come to take a look after the buffalo have passed by. We can't take a chance. We've got to pull out."

"But they're around us already," she chattered.

"We can still work our way clear to the north if we hustle," he said.

"We've got guns," she said. "We could stand off the Sioux if they came. Wouldn't we be safer staying here? Zack should be coming back any minute."

"Do you really believe that?"

"What else is there to believe?"

"He set this fire. He *wanted* the Sioux to see it and come here and kill us all, just like he let you and the wagons go ahead with so few men. He lied about the colonel at Miles saying the Sioux had signed treaty. He wanted you to be killed."

"Why would he want that?" she cried, agonized.

He took her arm, hurrying her down through the slants to their camp. "I don't know why he's doing this," he said. "Maybe to save his own skin. Maybe he figured to keep the Sioux busy so as to give him a chance to get clear. One thing's for sure. He knew the buffalo were coming. That's why he pulled out in the middle of the night before we were hemmed in."

They rushed into the camp and began frenziedly packing what food and utensils there were. Pedro was on his feet and dressed. "Are they coming?" he asked.

"All we could see so far are buffalo," Val said. "Can you ride? We can still get through to the north, with luck, but they'll have us blocked in all directions soon."

Sheila produced Pedro's rifle and six-shooter — and also the two weapons and the knife that Zack had taken from Val. "I — I kept them hidden," she confessed.

Val peered at her as he threw a hitch over the pack on the mule. "Why?" he asked.

"I — I thought it best," she said. She was garbing Penny.

"You don't seem to have trusted Zack too far after all," he commented.

"I knew something was wrong," she confessed. "It may be that he's gone insane."

"I doubt that," Val said. "It's something else. Why would he hate you enough to try to kill you."

"No!" she cried. "He wouldn't do that just because —" She didn't want to continue it.

"Just because what?"

"Because — because he asked me to marry him and I laughed at him," she said.

"I shouldn't have laughed at him, but the truth is I was always a little afraid of him."

"Being laughed at by a woman has led to murder plenty of times, I'm sure," Val said. "But it doesn't seem to be the answer this time. Zack just isn't the kind to risk being hung just because he didn't like being laughed at. And all this began long before you were old enough to think of marrying anyone. Eight years or more ago. He killed Boone and framed it on me. Now he's trying to fix it so the Sioux will kill you. Why? What's driving him?"

"I only wish I knew," she sobbed.

Val yanked the last hitch tight on the packmule and helped Sheila into the saddle of the horse she had been rigging with Pedro's help. He handed Penny up to her.

Pedro refused aid and mounted, hiding any pain the effort might have caused. Val led the way out of their redoubt. Little Penny uttered a cry of terror when they came in sight of the buffalo. Pedro clapped a hand over his mouth, the Yaqui sign of great awe and astonishment.

"Keep close to me," Val said. "Hold the horses down to a walk. No more talk. Don't make a sound. No sound at all. Just sit there like lumps."

He singled out an opening in the drifting

herd. Sheila followed with the child and Pedro brought up the rear, leading the mule.

Val felt tension in him as they neared the first buffalo. Some of the great beasts, mud-plastered, looking bigger than ever in their winter coats, lifted their heads and peered around, small eyes blinking. The black horse tossed its head and wanted to turn back, but Val patted its neck reassuringly and the black uneasily kept walking ahead.

Val, using knee pressure, guided the way between the groups of buffalo. The herd was not a compact mass, being composed of bands that evidently were under the domination of bulls, which grazed apart from each other. In places, some of the lanes and clearings were many rods in extent. However, the entire mass had a common purpose and a sort of cohesion. The great herd was creeping westward at a ponderous but uniform pace.

Buffalo were now all around them. Now and then an animal would show signs of alarm, toss its head and trot away from their path as they approached. These proved to be only individual movements. These alarms did not communicate to the main mass of the herd.

They could not hope to survive if a stampede started. Although they were moving through the thinner ranks of the advance guard of the herd on this north flank, they could see a great wing of advancing animals extending far to the northeast which they could not hope to outrun.

Val looked over his shoulder. Sheila had Penny gripped tight in her arms. She tried to smile weakly at him but it was only a grimace. Penny, now that they had made it this far, was beginning to brighten and gaze around wonderingly at the living menagerie. She wrinkled her nose in disdain at the animal odors that beset them.

Val chose the openings that offered the widest route. Behind them the finger of smoke still stood in the sky above the stand of rocks. He lifted in the stirrups, an inch at a time, peering ahead, hoping to see an end to their ordeal.

He halted his horse. A great bull, king of his band, had moved into their path and stood with horns lowered, eyes glaring wickedly.

Val had the rifle slung in his arm. He sat motionless, hoping the bull would not charge. In that case he would have to shoot. A gunshot would almost certainly trigger a stampede. Then they would have to ride the avalanche and hope to survive. A small hope at best.

Sheila and Pedro rigidly followed his example, sitting like statues. Even the horses and the mule seemed to sense that a wrong move now meant disaster. The bull pawed the earth, grunting angrily. But it was puzzled by the failure of this strange opponent to move. Val could feel the black horse go tense, preparing to whirl and dodge the attack if it came, just as it had learned to evade charging steers. He pressed a hand on its neck, holding it motionless.

The bull paused, snorting. Finally it turned and trotted away to rejoin its band. Val drew a long sigh. He heard Sheila breathing fast also.

"How much longer?" she murmured.

"Only a minute or two," he answered. "We're nearly there."

The sun was well up now in a hazy, cold sky that promised the return of rain or snow. He kneed the black horse ahead. Then the ranks of the buffalo thinned. Their path widened, became easier to follow without risk of exciting the animals.

Then they were clear! The thin brush line of the stream where Val had stalked the elk days ago showed ahead. They rode at a gallop now toward this offer of cover from any eyes that might be looking for them.

The stream proved to be a river of size instead of the creek they had expected. It wound through the bottom of a wide flood channel of boulders, driftwood and sand-flats with cutbacks that for long stretches would hide them. The stream was flowing from west to east at this point, and it was evidently rising, for its cold waters were carrying foam and mud.

They found a break in the cutbanks and descended into the bed of the river itself. A sound like the rising peal of thunder brought them standing in the saddle. The sound increased to a roar. The buffalo herd was stampeding!

Val, standing on the saddle peered over the rim of a cut-bank. The nearest buffalo were a considerable distance away on the flats and seemed to be swerving still farther southward from the river.

"We seem to be all right," he said. "Take a look!"

Even Penny scrambled to a vantage point to peer in awe at the flood of flesh that was rushing across the flats. Dust began to rise despite the cold. Here and there animals floundered and fell in bogs left by the rains and others piled on them.

It went on and on. On two occasions, wings of the stampede threatened to envelope even the river and Val gave the warning to be ready to ride. Each time the danger passed. Then it was over. The flats became vacant again, except for scattered animals that had been crippled or had failed to keep up.

Val said, "Look!"

The air beneath the overcast was very clear. The outcrop of rocks that had been their redoubt for days was sharply distinct four or five miles to the south. The thin wisp of smoke was still visible above it.

Something else moved there. Riders, small as insects at that distance, were swarming around the outcrop. Indians! Scores of them. The Sioux had seen the beacon and had come to investigate.

Sheila was staring, white-faced. "All right," Val said. "They can't be sure which way we went. The stampede has wiped out all tracks. We've got a long lead on them."

They rode up the riverbed. Val resisted the urge to push the horses, holding them down to a walk where the going was rough, letting them trot over the sandy stretches. At intervals he halted to take a look. On two occasions he sighted Indians, but they were far away and to the south.

"It's possible they might be more interested in making meat than taking scalps right now," he said. "They seem to be following the buffalo."

Twilight came, cold and raw. There was the promise of snow once again. Val prayed for snow, even with all its misery and discomfort. They had left a trail easy to follow. Snow might be their salvation.

Sheila was aware of this also. She lifted her arms to the sky in supplication. "Please, God, let it snow!" she said fervently. "Help us! Protect us!"

It did not snow. What came was another freezing, drenching rain. They left the river and camped in the lee of boulders. They huddled together beneath the tarps. Sheila and Val kept Penny between them, giving her what warmth they could from their own bodies. Pedro, proud and vain as ever, disdained showing any sign of weakness and toughed it out as best he could under the tarps.

"At least it'll be almost as good as snow if it keeps up," Val said. "It'll wash out our tracks."

They gnawed at stale biscuits and what scraps of jerky and meat left from the meals that Sheila had saved. The rain ended before daybreak and they continued their flight, keeping to what cover they could.

The Deadwood Trail was their hope of finding help. Just how far west it lay Val could only guess. He had hoped to find it at any moment, but realized that the meandering course of the river must have carried them north instead of west. There was no sun in the leaden sky that bridged the horizons and directions were also a matter of guesswork, with dependence mainly on Pedro.

Far to what Pedro said was west, they could see the outline of what apparently was rough country of buttes and ridges. The river now was perversely looping south again as though it was to find its way beyond the rough country. But the buffalo herd was somewhere south of them, and also the Sioux, no doubt.

They talked it over. The trail evidently had also swung farther west to avoid the broken country ahead. It was a choice of following the river and the relatively easy going, or fording it and chancing the passage of the rough country. They talked it over and decided on taking the latter course. At least the *malpais,* as Pedro pointed out, would give them a better chance to fort up and stand off the Sioux in case they were discovered.

However, fording the river offered a problem. The rains had speeded its rise. It was no longer the meandering stream almost lost in its wide bed. It had spread out, covering the biggest part of its flood channel and its main channel was a muddy, swift current. Yet cross it they must if they were to continue westward.

They rode for hours, hope fading in them. It was midafternoon when Val pointed. "There!" he said. The rising stream was spread from cutbank to cutbank, nearly half a mile wide, but it ran shallow, though swift, over what appeared to be a flat of bedrock. Except for the usual treacherous holes that could be located with poles of driftwood, the crossing appeared to be shallow enough to be feasible.

"I'm sure we can make it," he said, turning to them as they waited.

As he spoke his eyes picked out movement above the low cutbank far beyond them. Sioux. Mounted Sioux. At least a dozen of them. They were more than a mile away, but they were heading toward the river — directly toward the same ford they had just discovered.

It was evident the Sioux had not sighted them, hidden as they were by the river bank, for they were riding leisurely. But the Indians were sure to discover them if they continued on their present course.

Sheila and Pedro were unaware of what

Val had seen. They were still gazing dubiously at the wide expanse of water they were expected to cross.

"Keep going up the river!" Val said. "Don't try to cross here. At least now. Find cover if you can. Hide! If you can't, keep going. Fast. Find another ford. Above all, keep out of sight. I'll join you later."

"What's wrong?" Sheila cried.

"Indians!" Val said "Coming this way, probably to cross the river here. If we try to ford, they'll come up in time to see us and have us dead to rights. I'll go out there and try to decoy them into chasing me."

"But — but —" she began, horrified.

"I weel be the one!" Pedro exclaimed, and determinedly swung his horse to ascend out of the river bed.

Val seized the bit, halting the Yaqui's mount. "You will do better looking after the señorita and the *muchacha*," he said. "You know that. It is best that I try. I have the best horse. I can outrun them."

A faint smile of acknowledgment broke the granite-set of Pedro's face for an instant. He leaned forward, took Val's hands in both of his. "*Sí*," he said. "You are right. Go weeth God, *amigo*."

They sat looking deep into each other's eyes for a moment. "You no longer believe I killed Boone, do you, Pedro?" Val said.

"No, *amigo*," Pedro said. "I beg forgiveness for the wrong I did you. All of us here know who is guilty. But we still do not know why. It is more than the act of a jealous man. It is the act of *diablo* himself."

Sheila kneed her horse close. "Yes," she sobbed. "Can you ever forgive?"

She leaned from the saddle, placed her hands on his unshaven cheeks and kissed him. "We will pray for you," she said.

"Before you kiss me the next time," Val said, "give me a chance to shave first."

She tried to smile. "That's better," Val said, even though the smile was a failure. He wheeled his horse and headed away. "Keep going," he called back. "I'll find you. I'll find you."

She was not smiling. She was weeping. Penny, clutching her improvised doll, was crying also. "Don't go 'way, Mr. Man!" she wailed. "Come back! Come back!"

Val waved an arm. "Tomorrow, maybe, Penny. Maybe longer. But I'll come back!"

Pedro was punching the horses and the mule into motion when Val last looked back. After that the river's bank hid all sight of them. In spite of himself his eyes misted. He had to keep swallowing hard. He knew the odds were that none of them would ever see each other alive again.

The Sioux, if they were still heading for the ford, were hidden at the moment by a rise of land, but they would be less than half a mile away when they appeared and he estimated that he had less than five minutes leeway before he was sighted.

He urged the horse to a gallop, heading away from the river and angling slightly across the route by which the Indians would appear. After a minute or two he swung the black around, pulled it down to a walk and headed directly back toward the river. He wanted the Sioux to believe he had not yet reached the stream and was heading for the ford rather than having come from it.

The Sioux appeared at about the point he had expected. He pretended not to see them for a moment, although they were within long rifle range, keeping the black horse moving along at a walk.

From the corner of an eye he watched them. It was a bigger party than he had first estimated. There must have been nearly twenty of them. The majority were wrapped in blankets or buffalo robes or ponchos. Feathers fluttered from the heads of some. One wore a Texas cowboy's hat. That, no doubt, had belonged to Shorty Long or Miguel or the other *Si-Si* rider who had died at the wagons. Some of these then were among the braves who had kidnapped Sheila and Penny.

The Sioux halted their ponies instantly on sighting the lone rider on the flats between them and the river. They sat motionless for a space. Val knew they were examining the surroundings, making sure this was not a trap.

Someone must have given a command, for they hurled their ponies into motion. They made no sound, but Val knew that he dared wait no longer. He now acknowledged that he knew they were after him, and booted the black into full speed. He headed away from the river, cutting across their course somewhat. This brought him within shorter rifle range, but it was a risk that must be taken if his plan to decoy them succeeded.

The Sioux began yelling, almost gleefully. The chase was on. Some fired a few shots, but they did no damage and they quit wasting ammunition, waiting for the range to shorten more. Val veered more away from them, thereby offering a smaller target. He was beginning to lead them away from where he had left his companions.

The black horse was running easily, apparently not having suffered from its week of inaction in the hideout. Val gazed back, trying to estimate the quality of the mounts the Indians were riding. He lifted the rifle and fired two shots — more for moral effect and to warn them not to be too reckless.

In a typical maneuver, they were spreading out in a thin line. The warriors on the wings of the pursuit apparently were on the fastest ponies. The strategy was that of making him believe they were enveloping him so as to panic him into exhausting his mount by trying to outrun these flanking foes, even though they were actually not as close as the pursuers on the slower mounts astern.

The black was more than the master of the Sioux ponies. Val made flailing motions with arms and legs as though he had fallen for the Indians' ruse and was belaboring his mount into greater speed. None of his blows touched the black which was still not running at the pace of which it was capable.

Time was also in Val's favor. Misty twilight was already purpling the distant ridges of the west. His biggest danger now was that the black might fall, for it was running at a full gallop over rocks and spaces where there might be gopher or prairie dog holes. And he was still on the south or east side of the river, depending on the course of the stream, and somewhere in those directions were the buffalo herd and more Sioux, no doubt.

The Indians were now beginning to realize they were being outdistanced. Their ponies were beginning to fail, no doubt having seen hard use lately on the buffalo hunt. Val eased the black a trifle, wanting the Sioux to believe his own mount was failing also. That encouraged the pursuers to continue the chase a little longer. He judged that he had carried them nearly three miles from where he had left Sheila and the others. With darkness at hand they should have found a hiding place where they would be safe for the night at least.

He kept baiting the Sioux, keeping just tantalizingly within long rifle shot. Finally, on spent ponies, they gave it up. The last he saw of them they were turning back, beating the exhausted animals cruelly. He rode on through the deepening darkness, letting the black horse pick its own route. He finally let the animal halt and dismounted, rubbing it down as best he could with wisps of grass, then walked it slowly until it cooled before permitting it to graze. He listened in the chill early darkness, but the night was silent.

He doubted if the Sioux would attempt to trail him when daylight came. He had proved he was better mounted. He rode for another hour in darkness, heading back toward the river. At least he hoped that was the way he was heading for there were no stars, no guidepoints. He finally gave it up, and spent a bitter and dreary night with only his saddlecoat for protection. He arose at intervals to flail arms and legs to drive out the pervading chill.

At daybreak he climbed on foot to a ridge to study the country. As the light strengthened, scant spots of brush some three or four miles west of his position indicated that there lay the river. Somewhere along its course he might find them, or their trail.

He returned to his horse and headed for the river, keeping to hiding as much as possible. He halted suddenly, listening. He was sure he was hearing gunshots, but the sounds were so faint it was impossible to determine direction. The chances were the shots had come from the guns of Sioux, killing buffalo. At least that was what he hoped. He would not let himself think that Sheila might have been one of the targets.

He again tethered his horse and crawled to a rise. He lay there a long time, waiting. The rough terrain remained vacant. The course of the river was now little more than a mile away, so close he could see the muddy shine of the rushing torrent.

Then something moved in the flats nearer at hand. A single rider came in sight briefly, crossed an open stretch and vanished into the run of the country. At that distance Val could be sure of only one thing. The horseman was not an Indian.

Drearily he could only come to one conclusion. It must be Pedro Jaguar. Alone. Heading away from the river. He was thinking of the distant shots he had heard.

He saw the distant figure briefly again. He could not be sure, but it must be Pedro. Perhaps the Yaqui was still hunting a feasible ford by which he could get Sheila and the child across the river, and was seeking higher ground to get a look at the terrain.

With that hope buoying him, he returned to his horse and rode to intercept the lone man. He paused twice on rises, hoping to sight the mysterious rider again, but failed. He had been carrying the rifle, but when he returned to the horse he thrust it in the boot when he mounted. He headed down a swale between low ridges, expecting at any moment to encounter the man. He was successful. Rounding a stand of boulders he came face-to-face with a mounted man. But he was not Pedro. He was Zack Roper!

Zack had been waiting for him to come to

close quarters. For the second time Val found himself looking into Zack's six-shooter. This time Zack meant to kill him. Zack had the harsh, relentless light of murder in his eyes. He was mud-caked, wild-looking, but there was no fury in him. Nothing but impersonal coldness.

"Goodbye, Val," Zack said. "You've got more lives than a cat, but there's always a last one."

"Why, Zack?" Val said. He was helpless, and knew Zack meant to fire. His six-shooter was inside the buckled breast of his saddlecoat. A move toward the rifle would bring Zack's bullet. "Why did you kill Boone? Why have you tried to kill Sheila and the rest of us?"

"I ain't only tried, I've done it," Zack said. "I saw you get clear of the buffalo before they stampeded, so I followed you. I saw you draw off them Sioux an' that might have saved my scalp for they would have cut my trail, most likely. Sorry I can't repay the favor."

Zack fired. Val felt the hammer blow of the slug as it struck him in the chest. He knew he was toppling from the saddle. He believed he was a dead man.

10

✳✳✳✳✳✳✳✳✳✳✳✳✳✳✳✳✳✳✳✳✳✳✳✳✳

He began to try to swim, for he had the notion he was in the river. His efforts were feeble and he finally realized that it was raining again and that he lay in a chill puddle of water. He tried to move, but failed. He had trouble thinking. For a long time the vague thought was in his mind that he was paralyzed. He could not remember what had happened or how he had come to be here.

Sluggishly events began to take shape. Zack had shot him. He had felt the bullet strike. He remembered sinking into the blackness that he had thought was death. Gradually he gained more command of his body and of his thoughts. It was daylight, but whether it was the same day or not he had no way of telling.

From the position of the sun he began to realize it was not the same day. He must have lain there nearly twenty-four hours. The black horse was gone, along with the saddle and rifle.

He dragged himself to higher ground. Harsh pain nagged at him. He gradually realized that the bullet had struck the handle of the six-shooter he had been carrying in the breast of his saddlecoat. The force of the slug had been like the blow of a hammer not far from his heart. Perhaps he had lain there longer than a single day. Zack must have left him for dead or was sure exposure would finish him. Exposure or the Sioux.

Zack might still be right. Val felt more dead than alive. He managed to investigate his pockets. He had smoked his last cigarette days ago, but still had a supply of matches in a watertight case. He located the matches and found them dry. The day was nearing its end. Dusk was at hand, bleak and rainy.

He forced himself to start walking. That helped. It might have saved his life. He felt the numbness fade from his legs and feet and fingers as circulation strengthened. He began the process of living again. The pain of his bruised chest settled into a definite ache. He decided he might have a cracked rib or two. But he was alive. He intended to keep living. First he must look for Sheila. Or her body. Zack had said that he had killed her. Either way he would find out. Then he would look for Zack.

He managed to ignite a fire before dark among a small stand of brush and boulders, using gunpowder from one of the shells in his six-shooter to help get the twigs going. He nursed the blaze with all the skill Pedro had taught him until he could safely add to it. The fire might bring hostiles, but he could not live through the night without it.

No enemies came. Life returned completely as his body warmed. When daybreak came he set out to find Sheila. Reaching the river after two hours of walking through rain and mud, he found that the stream now was occupying its bed from bank to bank. The channel veered south and he followed it, for that was the way they would have gone if they had headed upstream to find another ford.

By midafternoon he was still plodding along the stream, keeping to cover when possible, but more often forced to move openly, hoping the weather would shield him from the eyes of any Sioux who might be around.

He finally realized that twilight was not far away. The rain had ended, but more might be on its way. He found that he was mumbling words. "Sheila! Sheila! Are you alive? Penny! Sweet, little Penny! What have they done to you?"

He was shocked into silence. He took a new grip on himself. Peering around he had the eerie feeling that he had seen all this before, and was only living over a nightmare that kept repeating itself. The low swells, the rounded hills, the rocky ridges, the loom of the *malpais* still far away in the misty light. It all seemed dreadfully familiar.

He realized he had seen all this before, and only that morning. Or had it been only in the morning? He was losing all track of time. He had traveled all day along a river over a great ox bow loop that had brought him back to less than a mile of his starting point. In all that day's bitter struggle he had found no track, no sign that any human being, mounted or on foot, had passed that way. He had not found Sheila.

He clutched at another hope. Perhaps they had found a ford downstream instead of up. If so, they might have crossed and by this time would have found their way west of the maze of loops the river made and be on their way to the *malpais*.

He began hurrying feverishly down the course of the river that had tantalized him. He began shouting loudly now, "Sheila! Sheila!"

There was no answer. He sighted something and broke into a stumbling run. Driftwood from both past and the present floods was lodged against the bank at the lower end of a bend. Wedged among the tangle was the carcass of a mule. It bore the *Si-Si* brand. It was the animal that had been carrying their camp pack.

Val, babbling Sheila's name, climbed among the driftwood and reached the carcass for a closer look. The mule had been shot through the head.

He arose, looking around with eyes that burned in his gaunt face. He saw something else lodged in the driftwood. A small item. A very small item. It was the doll that Sheila and Penny had improvised in their hidden camp from a stick of wood and rags.

He was remembering Zack's words about his attempts to bring about Sheila's death. "I not only tried, but I done it," Zack had said.

Val searched farther down the river, scanning every shallow and heap of driftwood and backwater. He kept it up until he could no longer see more than the glint of the muddy water in the last glimmer of the day. He found nothing more. The river rushed by, sounding its cold chuckling, its mocking, lonely laughter.

He sank down, burying his face in his hands. He wept.

Afterward he must have crawled to meager shelter and had fallen into a stupor. Death was near for him. It didn't seem to matter. Occasionally, whenever he drifted back to dim awareness of his loss and desolation, he would again mumble her name. "Sheila!"

Only the river answered.

He opened his eyes sluggishly to realize that a new day had come. The rain had ended. Wan sunshine touched him. He stared up into a circle of brown faces that looked down at him with curious dark eyes. Indians! He found himself trying to laugh mockingly, as the river had laughed. He had come full circle back to the beginning, just as he had stumbled along the river for a full day only to have it bring him to the starting point.

After all these days of hiding, of planning, of suffering, it was now over. He waited for the blow that would brain him. At least he would now be able to join Sheila.

The blow did not come. "He's a white man," a voice spoke. "By all that's holy I believe he's Dave Land! He's wanted for murder with a big price on his head. It looks like he's about done for."

A face came close over him, framed in the forage cap and hood of a cavalry officer. He knew that face. He had been acquainted with all the officers at Fort Miles. His mind was too numbed to think farther along that line. He realized that these Indians also wore items of army issue, along with their traditional buckskins and beads. They were members of the company of Crow scouts that was stationed at the post near Wagonbow.

The fragrance of food being cooked in army field pots was what first brought him back to reality. He found that he was lying in an army ambulance, wrapped in blankets. His clothing had been removed. A bandage was wound around his chest.

From beyond the canvas hood came the sounds of a military camp — men talking, laughter, rattle of tinware, stamping of hoofs. The aroma of tobacco smoke. He savored that. He had never before known how satisfying that could be. It assured him he was alive, back among his own kind.

Then he remembered: Sheila! Penny! Pedro! He tried to lift his head. It was too great an effort for a time. At last he succeeded. A wintry wind beat at the hood above him. He tried to call out but had to try several times before he could make a sound.

The wagon flap parted, the head of a soldier poked through. The head vanished and he heard the man say, "George, me boy, find the cap'n an' tell him the prisoner has opened his eyes."

Presently bootsteps came to the wagon and a man pulled himself through the flap into the interior. He was not the officer he remembered having seen with the Crow scouts. This one wore the bars of a captain on his overcoat. Joe Aberdeen was a cavalry captain stationed at Fort Miles and Val had played poker with him several times along with other officers at the post.

A second man pulled himself into the crowded vehicle, puffing and gasping with the effort. He was a civilian, bundled in a long wolfskin coat and a beaver fur cap. He was Henry Erskine, the Wagonbow banker. Jane's father.

Henry Erskine glared down at Val. "That's him all right, captain," he said. "He's lost a lot of weight an' looks like somebody cut off his beard with a hatchet an' it's just started to grow back. But that's him. Dave Land. I guess his real name is Valentine Lang."

Henry added, "Remember, Captain, I got first claim, an' aim to get it. I know my legal rights."

"That's none of the cavalry's business, nor mine," Aberdeen said curtly. "Now get

216

out. I want to talk to this man. Alone."

Henry hastily departed from the wagon, still grumbling about his legal rights. Joe Aberdeen looked down at Val and asked, "Are you able to talk?"

"Yes," Val mumbled. "Where are we?"

"Camped for a noon rest somewhere between hell and high water. On the Deadwood Trail in other words, about halfway to Fort Steele. We found you this morning lying out there half dead near a river the Crows say is a headwater of the Cheyenne. It was the Crows who found you rather, along with Lieutenant Curtis. They were scouting for sign of the Sioux. They brought you in on a travois about an hour ago. The company surgeon doctored that injury you have and a few other cuts and bruises. He says you probably have a cracked rib, but it might not be too serious."

"Sheila Irons?" Val croaked. "Penny? Pedro Jaguar?"

Aberdeen was startled. "You mean the young lady and the child who were taken from the wagons of that New Mexico outfit that was hit a week or so ago? Who's Pedro Jaguar?"

"My God, man, didn't you look for them? They might still be out there!"

"We have been looking for them,"

Aberdeen said. "That is why Bill Curtis and the Crows were scouting so far off the trail when they found you. We found this in your pocket. It looks like a doll the little girl might have had."

He showed Val the doll he had found lodged in the driftwood near the slain pack mule. "Where did you get this?"

Val and Joe Aberdeen had been friendly enough during poker sessions and had camped together on hunting and fishing trips. But the officer now was rigidly impersonal.

"I found it a day or two after I'd left them to try to decoy a Sioux hunting party away from them," Val said. "Look, Aberdeen, they may still be out there alive!"

"If so they may be found," Aberdeen said. "There's another detachment still out there with Crow scouts. However, they were given up days ago. The wagons with which they were traveling were found abandoned, all the men slain and the lady and the child missing."

"You'll keep with it until — until we know whether they're alive or dead?" Val asked desperately.

"I'm afraid we'll have to leave the search up to the detachment in the field," Aberdeen said. "I'm escorting half a dozen freight wagons and four or five settlers as far as Fort Steele. They're on their way to the Black Hills."

"What about Zack Roper?" Val asked. "Did the Crows find him too? Is he here in camp?"

"Zack Roper? That was the wagon boss of this *Si-Si* outfit from which the Irons girl and the child were stolen, wasn't it? He foolishly set out alone to trail them, so I understand. He's dead too, no doubt."

"What is Henry Erskine doing here?" Val asked.

"He's traveling with us as far as Fort Steele."

"Jane? Is she here too?"

"No. Miss Erskine is back in Wagonbow, of course. Her father has business in Fort Steele."

There was a silence. Aberdeen, of course, knew how it had been with Val and Jane Erskine.

"What about me?" Val finally asked.

"Is your name really Valentine Lang?"

"Yes," Val said.

"I understand you're wanted for murder," the officer said tersely. "Zack Roper and that New Mexican outfit wore everybody out around Wagonbow, looking for you. Roper even talked the colonel at the fort into loaning him some of the Crows and a platoon of troopers to try to find you. Roper says you murdered a young cattleman down there. He says you shot this man in the back."

"Then I'm under arrest?"

"You'll be held in custody until I can turn you over to a civilian officer of the law. There probably will be one at Fort Steele. At least a federal marshal."

"I'd prefer to be sent back to Wagonbow."

"That's impossible, of course. I'd have to send a strong escort with you. I can't weaken my force. The Crows say the country is full of sign of Sioux and Cheyenne hunting parties. Buffalo in considerable numbers too, and that's drawing the Indians. What difference does it make where I take you, now that you're in custody?"

"There's a person near this Fort Steele, so I understand, who has taken a vow to hang me with his own hands without giving me the benefit of the doubt, or a trial. His name is Cass Irons."

"I take it that he is the father of the man you murdered."

Val could see that Aberdeen had heard Zack's story and was taking it for granted that he was guilty. "I didn't kill Boone

Irons," he said. "But I know who did. And so does Sheila and Pedro Jaguar."

Aberdeen shrugged. "I'm afraid the chances are they are no longer alive."

"They were a day or two ago," Val said. "And so was Zack Roper."

"What?" Aberdeen demanded skeptically. "Are you sure?"

"I'm sure. I'll tell you the whole story, but you probably won't believe me."

"I've got a few minutes before we break camp," Aberdeen said. "I'll listen."

Val related what had happened from the night he fled from the tall house until the moment Zack Roper tried to kill him. He saw the incredulity grow in the officer's face. He shrugged when he finished. "You think I made that up, don't you, Joe?" he said wearily.

"You must admit yourself it sounds far-fetched," the officer said. "You are accusing this Zack Roper of murdering this Boone Irons and hanging the crime on you. Then Roper, years later, tries to fix it so that a woman and a child and this Yaqui are massacred by Indians. Then he tries to kill you in cold blood."

"Exactly."

"Is the man insane?"

"Not as far as I could see," Val admitted.

Aberdeen was puzzled. "Your story lacks one item. An important one. A motive. What reason would Roper have for such crimes unless he was demented?"

"I don't know," Val said.

"To tell you the truth, Land, or Lang, whichever name is correct, I couldn't help being impressed by what you just told me. It was so fantastic the thought struck me that you couldn't have made it up out of whole cloth. At least you told it well." He added, "But I doubt if a jury would ever believe it."

"It won't get to a jury," Val said. "Cass Irons will take care of that."

"I'm sure the law will see that you get a fair trial," Aberdeen said. "But I doubt that anyone will believe that a man wanted for the murder of one member of a family would risk what you say you did for Miss Irons and the child. In addition, they apparently are your only witnesses in your behalf. And the odds are that they are dead."

He paused for a moment, then added, "They could also have been the only witnesses *against* you at a trial."

Val stared at him. "You think I murdered them?" he breathed. "To see that they never testified against me?"

"I didn't say that," Aberdeen said. "I merely wanted to see your reaction. To tell you the truth I don't believe anything like that. Bill Curtis tells me you did some raving after they found you. In fact, although he didn't get much coherent out of you, what he told me about your words sort of fit in with your story. In addition you kept saying that Zack Roper murdered Sheila Irons. You also kept saying that you were in love with her."

"A man says things in fever that would be better not mentioned," Val said.

"What about Jane Erskine?"

Val eyed him stonily and did not answer.

"I'm not prying into your private life without a reason," Aberdeen persisted. "For one thing a man would hardly murder a girl he raved about being in love with."

"Thanks. Is that a point in my favor?"

"Perhaps. But weren't you and Jane Erskine to have been married? At least that was common knowledge around Wagonbow?"

"That was over the night I had to run for it when Roper and the *Si-Si* crew came for me and burned the new house."

"Do you know why Miss Erskine's father is on his way to Fort Steele with us?" Aberdeen asked slowly.

"I have no idea." Then Aberdeen's expression told him the truth. He rose to an elbow. "It couldn't have been her? Not Jane?

223

Not for the reward?"

"I'm sorry," Aberdeen said. "Erskine is going to Fort Steele to find this man, Cass Irons, and claim $10,000 reward in his daughter's name. Apparently she went to Zack Roper in Wagonbow that night and told him who you really were and where he could find you."

The silence went on and on. "I'm sorry," Aberdeen finally said. After a moment, he added, "There's still hope. As I told you a detachment, under Lieutenant Harker, is making a sweep through the country east of here. Harker has Crows with him and they may find trace of Miss Irons and the other two. Harker will rejoin us at Fort Steele."

Val still did not answer. Jane had betrayed him for money. After the first shock of bitterness had passed he began to realize it hardly mattered. It occurred to him that Jane had not entered his thoughts for days. There had never been real love between them, only a desire on her part to marry a man her father said would some day be wealthy, on his part to find a companion to end his loneliness.

Aberdeen left the wagon. An orderly brought food, but Val was unable to eat. Camp was broken and the afternoon march began. He lay, bracing himself as the vehicle lurched over the rough trail. A trooper sat on the seat with the driver, a carbine across his knees, a pistol handy. The man had been detailed to see that he did not try to escape.

When the night camp was made more food was brought. This time he forced himself to eat. Nourishment did wonders for him. The lethargy and weakness of body and spirit faded. He cleaned the mess tin and asked for more.

It was Aberdeen himself who brought the refill. "You've got a lot of meals to catch up on," the officer remarked.

"How far did you say it was to Fort Steele?" Val asked.

"About eighty miles, I'd say. We ought to make it in less than three days, provided the freighters can handle the trail. We've hit some muddy traveling."

Val looked around. "My clothes?"

"The ones you were wearing weren't of much use. I'll see what I can do."

He left and returned after a time with clean underwear, a woolen shirt and breeches, along with cowhide boots of the type the freighters wore, and a cavalry jacket.

"Whose debt am I in?" Val asked.

"The muleskinners, mostly," Aberdeen said. "The jacket is one of my spares."

"I'll speak to Henry Erskine," Val said. "I've got an account in his bank. He can pay you and the skinners."

"I personally don't care for any money that Erskine has handled," Aberdeen said.

"I didn't kill Boone Irons," Val said. "I wasn't too sure of it myself until lately. Now I know beyond all question I didn't. Zack must have slipped something into one of those few drinks I had. And Boone's too, maybe. He got my gun from me after I got on my horse to ride home and killed Boone with it, planting marks of corduroy in the sand. Then he put the gun back on me while I was sleeping it off. I know now that I couldn't have killed Boone. A man doesn't do things that are against his nature, no matter if he was drunk."

"That's not for me to decide," Aberdeen said. "It'll be up to a jury."

"Up to Cass Irons, I'm afraid," Val said.

11

After Aberdeen left, Val dressed in the borrowed garb. Every fiber in his body seemed stiff and aching. The bandaged injury throbbed, marking the spot where Zack's bullet had come within an ace of killing him.

He lowered himself from the wagon to the ground. Full darkness had come and fires lighted the camp. He found himself looking into the muzzle of a carbine held by a cavalryman. "Halt!" the man said. "I've got orders not to let ye leave the wagon widdout the cap'n's permission."

Aberdeen who had been drinking coffee with other officers at a campfire, came walking up. "I'll walk with him, private," he said. "You might follow us at ten paces. He needs a little exercise."

Val and the officer walked through the camp. It was a sizable outfit. Laden prairie wagons had been set in the frontier circle for defense. The cavalry camp enclosed the open end of the circle. The stable line was close by and heavily guarded against the possibility of a raid. The Crows had set up a camp of their own and were dipping into steaming pots, fishing out edibles which they ate with bare fingers, obviously enjoying the fare.

"Prairie dog stew," Aberdeen said disdainfully. "It's enough to turn a man's stomach."

"In some places they're called prairie squirrels," Val said. "They taste mighty good when a man's really hungry. Only the name's against them."

"You've eaten those things?"

"Boone and I got caught on dry stretches a time or two on the Staked Plains when we were trying to get us a buffalo. We had our choice between them or rattler meat, because we didn't see hide nor hair of buffalo."

"You and this man, Boone Irons, must have really been close friends if you were hunting partners on trips like that."

"Yeah," Val said. "Mighty close. There was another time when we bagged a buffalo. A big bull. Must have weighed close to a ton. It must have been over a hundred in the shade and you don't find much shade up on the *Estacado*."

He went on to relate their tribulations in trying to take the hide and head of the kill.

What he was doing was talking to keep Aberdeen off guard. He was appraising the cavalry stable line. The sentries were on post beyond the camp. Saddled horses for a squad were picketed inside the camp so that mounts would be available in case the Sioux succeeded in stampeding the remuda — a maneuver that had often left cavalry outfits afoot when they lacked mounts to round up scattered animals.

"I better head back to bed," Val said. "I'm not as up to it as I thought."

"I'm posting a sentry to see that you don't walk in your sleep," Aberdeen warned. "It's my duty. These men have itchy trigger fingers. They always have in hostile country. We lost half a dozen men on our last trip up this road when a big bunch of Sioux and Cheyennes hit us. There's a rumor around that you might not be exactly on our side."

"What does that mean?" Val demanded.

"You looked pretty wild when you were brought in," Aberdeen said. "Some of the men seem to think you smelled like you'd been in an Indian village."

This time Val gave way to the helpless, bitter laughter that was building up in him. They suspected that he was not only a fugitive but that he might have turned renegade.

"Maybe they think I might be here to

bring the Sioux down on them," he said jeeringly.

Aberdeen was grimly silent. It was plain that after he had time to think it over and discuss it with other officers he had swung back to his first conviction that Val's story could not be believed. Apparently he considered it within the bounds of possibility that Val had thrown in with the hostiles against his own kind.

As they headed for the army ambulance Val found himself confronted by Henry Erskine, who had popped out of one of the freight wagons where he evidently was taking shelter.

"Hello, Henry," Val said. "Think of seeing you here on your way to try to collect $10,000 on my scalp."

"Don't talk to me like that, you scoundrel!" Henry stuttered. "You broke my daughter's heart, leadin' her to believe you was a respectable, upright man, when all the time you was a murderer an' an outlaw with a price on your head."

"Maybe you've really earned that $10,000, Henry," Val said. "Or does it all go to Jane? I imagine you're doing pretty well without it. How many of my cattle and horses have you hired the riffraff to steal by this time? I suppose you're fixing to get your hands on all the land I owned. Is that right?"

"I'm arrangin' to have myself appointed administrator of whatever property you had, so as to protect your interests an' that of the state," Henry said pompously. "You'll get what's comin' to you after all costs are taken care of."

"I'll make a bet that there won't be much left for the state or anyone else after you get through lining your pockets, Henry."

"There'll be enough to bury you," Henry sniffed.

"I'm not dead yet," Val said.

"You soon will be. Them that hangs out with savages git no mercy in these parts."

"Are you the one that put that bee in their bonnets about me having thrown in with the Sioux?" Val demanded.

"It was plain enough for everybody to see. Wasn't you the one that was found with the doll that belonged to that poor murdered child? How did you come by that 'less you was in it with the Indians?"

"So you *are* the one," Val said. "I see your point. You figure nobody will object much to you stealing the property of a renegade. The blacker I'm painted the better."

"You're a fine one to preach," Henry jeered. "You what tried to lure my daughter into sharin' your iniquity. Cass Irons' nephew told me all about you an' how you waylaid his cousin an' murdered him just because he was a better man than you. He told —"

"Hold on!" Val exclaimed. "What was that? Cass Irons' nephew? What are you talking about."

"I'm talkin' about the man what's range boss of *Si-Si*. Him an' me had a long palaver back in Wagonbow after Jenny Jane went to him and exposed you for what you are. He told me how you murdered his cousin down there in New Mexico."

"Are you talking about Zack Roper?"

"I ain't talkin' about nobody else. He told me he knew you when you was a tad, an' that you never was no good."

"Let's get this straight," Val said wildly. "Zack Roper told you he was Cass Irons' nephew?"

"That's what I'm sayin'," Henry declared. "He was the adopted son o' Cass Irons' sister. Cass Irons took him into his family as a foster nephew."

Val stood staring at Henry for a long time. He was not seeing him. He was seeing a lot of things far away that he had not been able to explain. Now the explanations were clear and brutal.

"So that's it?" he breathed. *"So that's it?"*

He grasped Henry by the front of his wolf-skin coat and shook him. "Are you lying, Henry? If so I'll tear your tongue right out of you. Tell me again. Zack said he was the foster nephew of Cass Irons? He really told you that?"

"Let go o' me!" Henry screeched. "Cap'n, don't let him hurt me. O'course he told me. He more'n told me. He put it in his will."

"His will? Zack Roper's will? How do you know that?"

"I made it out for him, that's how. Jane an' John Wink witnessed it. Zack Roper figured he'd better make out his will before he went out to hunt you down. He left everything he owned in this world to be divided between his foster uncle, Cass. C. Irons an' his cousin, Sheila Irons."

Val was remembering snatches of bunk-house gossip he had heard among old-timers when he had been riding for the *Si-Si*. They had seemed unimportant at the time and he had put it down to the human tendency to try to drum up scandal when there really was none.

Now he began recalling the vague hints and sly innuendos that Cass Irons had an older sister who had eloped with a worthless tinhorn gambler when she was a young girl and had led a lurid life. It had been said that

233

she had died after a few years of dissipation in a bawdy dive across the border in Mexico. There had been stories that the tinhorn had a son by a former marriage whom Lucinda Irons had adopted and raised as her own child until she had been hit by a stray bullet during a drunken gunfight between Rurales and the tequila-filled patrons at the *cantina*. Her tinhorn husband had long since deserted her and vanished.

Val began recalling other things from the past, small items that now began to have significance. For one thing, Zack had been given an amazing amount of authority at the big C-Bar-C. He had free run of the main house, although he also had been given comfortable separate quarters in a house that had been built for him by Cass Irons — a concession that no other range boss at *Si-Si* had enjoyed, not even Val's father.

He saw it all now. Case Irons, with his stubborn, patrician pride, had kept secret the fact that his own sister had stained what he considered the family honor by running away with a cheap gambler and had died in a low dive on the border. Apparently Cass Irons had taken his sister's foster child under his wing and raised him to manhood, making him range boss of *Si-Si* and giving him great authority in return for a pact between them that the stain on Cass Irons' proud family name would never be revealed. Val believed that even Sheila had not known of this connection with the family by Zack.

Henry Erskine was scowling under Val's blank stare, not realizing that he was not even being seen. "What's wrong with you?" the banker stuttered. "Why you lookin' at me like that? Have you gone dippy?"

"How blind I've been!" Val said hoarsely. "How blind was Sheila."

He gazed at Henry. "He must have killed Wyatt, too," he said. "He must have fixed the cinches on Wyatt's saddle so they'd bust. And he murdered Boone. But why did he wait so long? Eight years or more. Why?"

"What're you talkin' about?" Henry mumbled.

"Zack's smart," Val said. "That was a real smart thing when he made out that will. He's got legal proof he's Cass's loving nephew. He thinks so much of his foster uncle and his cousin Sheila he's leaving everything he owns to them if something happens to him. Now, that's real clever, real touching."

"If'n you ask me, he done the right thing," Henry squeaked. "Chances air he's dead now. He done a mighty brave deed, settin' out alone to trail them Sioux thet had stole his cousin an' the little girl. If he's dead, I'll see to it that his uncle — or his cousin if she's alive — gits the benefit of his estate."

"I doubt that Zack had much in the way of an estate to leave to anybody," Val said. "A horse and saddle, maybe. A poker deck. It likely had marked cards. He played with crooked cards most of his life, it seems."

"That's no way to talk about a man what's likely dead," Henry whined. "No matter how little a man owns he's entitled to leave it to them he thinks deserves it. It looks to me like he had a premonition when he made out that will."

"A premonition that would help him inherit an estate worth upward of a million," Val said. "Maybe more. I'm beginning to understand why Zack worked so hard, took such long chances. A million dollars' worth of cattle ranch is quite a reward."

"I don't know what you're talkin' about," Henry said.

"I'm sure you do," Val said. "In the back of that mind of yours you already see the light, because it's the sort of scheme you could appreciate."

He turned to Captain Aberdeen. "The skunk smell around here is getting a little too much. Let's move."

With the guard following, he returned to the ambulance. He suddenly pretended dizziness and weakness and Aberdeen helped him into the vehicle, helped strip off his clothing and rolled him into the blankets. Aberdeen called the company doctor who arrived, smelling of whisky and grumbling his opinion of renegades who didn't deserve help. The man made a pretense at taking Val's pulse and rolling back his eyelids, while peering over a lighted match, but it was all perfunctory, and he left still disgruntled at having been called away from the conviviality around the officers' fire.

Val lay there, waiting. He heard the second guard being posted. For lack of a bugler the officer of the day walked through the camp calling out vocally, "Taps! Turn In! Turn In. We march at daybreak. Taps!"

Soon, except for the muted call of the sentries keeping in touch with each other, the camp was asleep. Val continued to wait. At midnight a sergeant aroused the change of guard. There was muted activity for a time. Then the camp slept again.

Val bided his time, giving the new sentries time to become bored and drowsy with their cold duty. He finally rolled out of his bed, dressed silently and pulled on the dog-eared boots. He crept to the flap, parted it cautiously enough for an eyehole. As Aberdeen had said, a sentry was on duty at the wagon to see that he did not try an escape. But the trooper was walking his beat like a man in a dream, more asleep than awake.

The saddled horses were faint shadows against the background of bulking freight wagons. The embers of the dying fires were fanned to life occasionally by gusts of the cold wind. He moved to the front of the wagon, slid over the driver's seat and reached the ground in silence.

He moved through the camp and reached the horse string unchallenged. Earlier in the evening he had singled out a rangy, long-legged roan as probably the best of the lot. This was the animal whose reins he now freed from the line.

The soil underfoot was spongy. The roan's hoofs made little sound as he led it cautiously deeper into the shadow of a wagon. He waited there, peering in the faint fireglow, deciding his next move.

He was unarmed. Not far away carbines were stacked temptingly in front of a bivouac where troopers snored. They were single-shot Springfield carbines with cartridge boxes hanging nearby. However, more to Val's preference was a magazine Winchester, which had been placed leaning against the wall of a tent. This evidently was the weapon of a buckskin-fringed civilian scout whom Val had seen in the camp.

He appropriated the rifle, started to steal away into the shadows, heading toward the waiting roan horse. He paused, struck by a new thought. His first plan had been to mount a horse and try to ride past the sentries, gambling on the hope of getting away without being hit, for he was sure to draw fire.

He eyed the cartridge boxes and belts near the stacked Springfields. One of the campfires was still crimson, the embers fanned by the gusts of night wind. He made his decision, crawled back and tossed one of the boxes of cartridges into the coals.

He retreated to where the roan stood. He had only seconds to wait. The shells began to explode in the fire, the reports startlingly loud in the night.

"Indians!" Val yelled. "Indians! Indians!"

He swung into the saddle and spurred the horse toward the sentry line. "They're coming at us from the other side of camp," he screeched.

Two of the sentries ran confusedly past him into the camp where the shells were still exploding and bullets whizzing. Val kept riding ahead, away from the camp. The uproar continued back of him until distance drowned it out.

He was now riding to save Cass Irons' life.

12

✳✳✳✳✳✳✳✳✳✳✳✳✳✳✳✳✳✳✳✳✳✳✳✳✳

Aberdeen had said that Fort Steele lay some eighty miles farther up the trail. North. Val singled out the Big Dipper in the misty sky. He remembered what Pedro called it. *El Reloj de los Yaquis* (Clock of the Yaquis). He sighted along its pointers and located Polaris, the North Star.

No doubt the captain would send some of the Crows in pursuit. He followed the timber and ridges for a time, then swung back to the road for the sake of better going, letting the roan set its own pace.

When daybreak came he left the road and traveled more slowly and cautiously, keeping to cover, for the Crows were only one of the dangers now. Twice he crossed sign of Indian hunting parties, but the evidence was more than a day old at least. However, it was proof there could be others.

The roan tired suddenly late in the afternoon and began to favor its right rear leg. He was forced to throw off for the night, making a cold and cheerless camp in timber. The animal's injury was dispelled by the night's rest, but it had lost its zest for travel and was turning out to be hard-mouthed and obstinate.

The distant report of the sunset gun told him that he was at last nearing his destination. He halted in the edge of the clearing and dismounted, gazing out at Fort Steele. It stood in a flat from which the timber had been cleared. Tree stumps studded the area around the stockade. Sentries stood at the opened log gates and the heads of more showed on the firing steps.

A settlement had sprung up near the fort. Log-built houses, jerry-built shacks, corrals were huddled around the block-long heart of the town through whose muddy street the Deadwood Trail made its way and plunged into timber beyond. Smoke rose from chimneys, lamplight was beginning to glint.

Val dismounted among the trees and appraised the situation. He waited until twilight had deepened, then mounted the tired roan and circled the settlement, entering it on the trail from the north.

The biggest structure in Fort Steele housed a trading post. Bearskins, wolf pelts and buffalo hides were stacked on its platform, protected by tarps. It was still open for business, and he could see a bearded man dickering with a customer.

Next door was a rude saloon, its shake roof crooked, its slab door hung on leather hinges. Lamplight showed through a window that had not been washed in months if ever.

He dismounted, tethered the horse and entered the saloon. He was famished, and evidently the place provided food as well as liquor, for the aroma of meat being cooked came from the door that led to a kitchen at the rear.

"I need grub," Val said to the bartender.

"I reckon you do, from the looks," the man said. "Got any money?"

"No," Val said. "But you'll be paid. I have to get in touch with a cattleman named Cass C. Irons. It's important. I understand he's setting up a ranch near here. I —"

The barkeeper's attention had slid past him to the only other patron in the room. This man had been sitting apparently asleep in a chair tilted against the wall with his hat pulled over his eyes.

Val heard the legs of the chair thump to the floor. The muzzle of a pistol was jammed into his back. Zack Roper's voice said, "You're a tough man, Val. I thought I had left you for dead days ago."

Val expected to be shot, but the bullet did

not come. Zack ran hands over him, searching for a pistol. Finding none, he stepped back. Val turned. Zack was gaunt-faced, his growth of whiskers matted, his eyes red with exhaustion.

"I've been waitin' for you, Val," he said. "I only got here an hour or so ago. I just about rode a horse to death to git here ahead of you."

"You *knew* I was still alive?" Val asked.

"I came onto that cal'vry outfit the mornin' after you'd flew the coop along with a government horse an' a rifle. The captain was fit to eat nails. I told him I had a hunch where I could set a deadfall for you an' talked him into givin' me a fresh horse in place o' the one I was ridin' which was pretty well wore out."

"Why did you think I'd come here?" Val asked.

"To kill Cass Irons, o' course," Zack said. "An' me. We're the only ones left that could put your neck in a noose, now that all the others are dead."

"So Sheila is dead?" Val said. "So you did kill them that day at the river? And you also murdered Boone? Did you cause Wyatt's death too?"

Zack, without taking his eyes off Val, addressed the bartender. "Listen to him," he said. "Clever, ain't he? Slippery as an eel. He's murdered three or four people in cold blood and now he's come here to kill me an' Cass Irons so we can't ever testify against him. And he stands there tryin' to make out I was the one that done it."

Val still expected to be killed. "Go ahead, Zack," he said. "You can't miss. You didn't miss the other time, but I was lucky. They won't hang you any higher for one more, but the devil might think of something special for you. You can't take the *Si-Si* with you when you go, you know. And you will go some day. Everybody does."

Still Zack did not trip the trigger. Instead, he lowered the hammer. Before Val knew what was coming next Zack took a stride, swinging the muzzle of the six-shooter and brought it against his temple.

He felt himself falling, saw the floor coming up to meet him. Then a plunge into blackness.

The next thing he heard was the bartender's voice. "Looks like you won't have to bother stringin' him up, Mr. Roper. Chances air you cracked his skull. I ain't blamin' you for lettin' him have it. A man what done all you just told me he done ain't fit to live."

"He's got to live long enough for Cass

Irons to see him," Zack said. "Fetch some water. And a slug of whisky. That'll bring him around, maybe."

Val felt his hair being seized roughly and his head lifted. Water was dashed in his face, then whisky was poured into his mouth, gagging him. Enough of it reached his stomach to form a little pool of warmth.

"He's all right," Zack said. "Snakes don't die that easy."

"There's an army doc at the fort," the bartender said. "Maybe we better fetch him."

"He don't need a doctor," Zack said. "I didn't hit him that hard. I'm takin' him out to the ranch so Cass can see the man what murdered his kinfolk. Did you say Cass's new spread is only about three miles out? Just how do I get there?"

"Just foller the road north. You'll come out o' the timber after a mile or so an' into open country. Not far beyond you'll see the new buildin' off in a flat to the left. There's a sign at the fork. You just can't go wrong. But wouldn't it be better if you turned this feller over to the law? There's a deputy U.S. marshal stationed here. He's likely up at the fort right now chewin' the fat with the officers or playin' cards."

"We'll worry about handin' him over to the marshal later," Zack said. "Cass has turned heaven an' hell to find this man. He gits first crack at him."

"Lawsie, you don't think Mr. Irons would string him up do you?" the bartender said uneasily.

"I wouldn't blame him if he did," Zack growled. He dragged Val to his feet. "Git goin', you!" he snarled. "Don't try to play possum with me. We're takin' a little ride. We're on our way to see an old friend o' yours."

Val reeled dizzily, but Zack shoved him through the door into the cold outer air and to the side of his horse. "Git on it!" he said. "That horse looks plenty weary but I reckon it can stand a few more miles."

He prodded Val into the saddle. Val managed to find the stirrups. His head began to clear rapidly.

"Just you sit there tight!" Zack warned. "Barkeep, you blast him to mincemeat if he tries to git away. I'm goin' over to the livery an' get me a horse. Mine ain't even good for three miles."

The bartender was standing in the door of the saloon, a double-barreled shotgun in his hands. He swung the gun around, covering Val. Three or four citizens, attracted by the loud voices, arrived and stood staring.

Zack returned after a few minutes,

mounted on a young, nervous horse. "Take a good look at this man, my friends," he told the bystanders. "He's wanted for murder down in New Mexico. He murdered a young lady and a child not long ago because they would be witnesses against him. And he came here to kill the father of the victims so that there'd be nobody alive to bring him to justice. He didn't count on me. I'm a nephew of Cass Irons, who he came here to kill. I'm takin' him out to Cass's place now an' will let Cass hear the story from his own lips."

"Better take that carbine off'n his saddle, Mr. Roper," the bartender said. "If'n I was you, I'd tie him to thet horse to make sure —"

Zack didn't seem to hear. He brought the reins of his own mount down on Val's horse, startling it into a gallop. He struck his own mount with the reins. "Don't try to make a run for it, Val!" he warned. "I'll kill you if you do!"

Zack's mount suddenly went to pieces. It bowed its back and went buck-jumping and sunfishing in the muddy street. Zack was nearly unseated.

Val's horse, panicked by the commotion, broke into a wilder gallop, leaving Zack behind, trying to hang onto the saddle of his bucking mount.

"He's gittin' away!" Zack shouted. "Stop him!"

"I'm feared o' hittin' you, if I shoot, Mr. Roper!" the bartender shouted. "He's out o' sight! It's too danged dark!"

The roan carried Val out of the settlement and along the trail into the timber. He presently swung the animal off the trail and pulled it to a stop.

After a minute or two he heard a horse speed past on the road. That undoubtedly was Zack, who was staging a pursuit now that he had subdued his mount.

Val suddenly understood. Zack had planned the whole thing. He had gigged his horse into going to pieces in order to let Val escape. He had deliberately overlooked the carbine on the saddle of Val's mount. He had wanted Val to be armed.

Val urged the roan back onto the road and headed in the direction Zack had been riding. According to what he had heard the bartender say the new *Si-Si* ranch was in this direction and not too far away now.

He encouraged the tired roan to do its best. The army post appeared to the left and fell behind. A few lights burned there. The muddy softness of the trail muffled the sound of the animal's hoofs.

Zack could be no more than a minute or

two ahead of him, but being on a fresher mount, probably was pulling farther in the lead. Or he might be waiting in ambush, for he would surely know that Val would be heading for the *Si-Si* also. Val doubted that. Zack had another matter to take care of first. Cass Irons was at the *Si-Si,* and Zack was on his way to murder him as he had murdered the others.

The roan began to fade. Abruptly it carried Val clear of the blackness of the timber. Open flats lay ahead. The lights of a ranch appeared off the road — small red dots that came from the windows of buildings.

Val halted his mount. It was blowing hard. He dismounted and walked away from it, taking the carbine with him. Now he could hear the distant sound of another horse that had been hard-run. The animal had halted, for there was no sound of hoofs. Crouching, watching the skyline of stars, after a tense wait Val glimpsed the shadow of a man on foot moving between him and the lights of the ranch.

13

✳✳✳✳✳✳✳✳✳✳✳✳✳✳✳✳✳✳✳✳✳✳✳✳

Val moved ahead, trying to be as silent as possible. The lights came nearer and now he could make out the outline of a log-built house. Flanking it were new pole corrals, the shape of a shed, and tents that evidently were temporary quarters for the crew.

Once more he sighted the shadow moving between himself and the house. He levered a shell into the firing chamber of the carbine. The metallic sound was loud in his own ears.

Zack must have heard it also, for the shadow Val was tracing, vanished. All Val could hear was the sound of his own heartbeat. He could picture Zack crouching in the darkness, trying to locate him.

He knew he was playing Zack's game. Zack *wanted* him here, close at hand when Cass Irons was murdered. The circle would be complete. The last of the Irons would be dead and their murders placed at Val's door.

He heard Zack moving, fast. The big man

had abandoned stealth. The trap had been set, the scene cunningly staged and now he meant to drop the final curtain.

Val ran ahead also. The smell of freshly logged pine timber filled the night. The corral, with its spidery legs barred his path and he had to detour around it, agonized by this delay.

The main house loomed ahead, less than a hundred yards away. One wing was still unfinished and roofless but lamplight glowed in windows of the occupied section.

"Cass! Cass Irons!"

Zack had lifted the shout, using a shrill falsetto to disguise his voice. He was crouched somewhere in the darkness and Val knew he had a gun in his hand and ready.

"Cass! Cass Irons!" Again he lifted the weird shout.

Val heard footsteps in the house as though someone was hurrying to open a door. He lifted his own voice. "Stay there, Cass! Don't open that door! You'll be killed!"

Gun flame erupted from the shadows to his right. The bullet struck a post of the corral beyond him. Zack had been closer than he had believed. The big man had been forced to turn his gun on Val, knowing now that he must be silenced if his years of scheming were to pay off.

That was Zack's mistake. His first real error. He had panicked at the final moment. He had exposed his own position.

Val lifted the carbine and fired four times, raking the area from which the shot had come. He heard one of his bullets find flesh. The sound was like the rending of cloth. He heard Zack utter a moan, heard him writhing in the grass.

He ran forward and found Zack still twisting in agony. Zack still had his six-shooter in his hand. He tenaciously tried to lift it and shoot, tried to salvage something from the wreck of his plans. Val kicked the gun from his hand.

Cass Irons came running from the house. He was in shirtsleeves and had a six-shooter in his hand. Other hurrying footsteps sounded as the crew poured from the tents and came racing to the scene. Someone brought a lighted lamp.

"I'm Val Lang," Val said.

"I know who you are," Cass Irons said.

"I just shot Zack Roper," Val said. "You better get him into the house and send for a doctor. He came here to kill you and make it look like I did it. Just like he killed Boone. And maybe Wyatt too. Like he fixed it so the Indians would get rid of Sheila and your grandchild. He wanted *Si-Si* for himself. He'd be your only heir. It seems that he claims to be your nephew."

He didn't expect Cars to believe him. He waited for the grim cattleman to shoot him. Instead, Cass ran an arm around him. "My God, Val, my God!" Cass said. "Will you ever forgive me?"

A girl came racing. Val found himself looking into a face he had never expected to see again. A face from the grave. Sheila!

She was no ghost. She was alive! Her face was thin and drawn. Like his own. Her eyes were deep wells between high cheekbones. She was beautiful, the most wonderful sight he had ever seen.

"Val!" she sobbed. "Oh, my dear!" She put her arms around him, drew him against her. "You're safe, you're safe."

"I was blind," her father said. "Why I didn't know from the first it was Zack I'll never figure out, I reckon. It should have been plain enough."

Val's confused eyes saw the seamed face of Pedro Jaguar in the circle. He was holding Penny in his arms. Penny was thin-faced also, but neatly dressed, her hair combed. Like her aunt, she was weeping. But they were tears of joy. "I'm so glad you came back, Mr. Man," she wailed.

It was many minutes before Val could really believe it. By that time they were in the new ranchhouse with its bare floors, its need of a woman's touch to bring it to life.

Zack had been carried in and lay now on a cot. The bullet had drilled through his body. He was still alive, and Pedro Jaguar's first diagnosis was that he would pull through. A rider was already on his way to the army post to bring the doctor.

"Crow scouts for a cavalry outfit under a nice officer named Lieutenant Harker found us," Sheila said. "They were sent out to hunt the Indians who had ambushed our wagons. The Sioux kept out of their way, of course, so they came on through to Fort Steele. We arrived yesterday. I asked the cavalry to keep quiet about having found us."

"Why?"

"After they heard my story they agreed. For one thing we knew you were alive. Lieutenant Harker was keeping in touch with the troops escorting the wagon train. The Crows were carrying dispatches back and forth. We learned that you had been captured, then had escaped. Also that Zack had shown up alive and that he was riding ahead, trying to overtake you before you reached Fort Steele."

"The river?" Val exclaimed. "I found

Penny's doll. I found the mule shot. I searched for miles for your bodies."

"We were fording the river when Zack started shooting," she said. "I suppose he had been trailing us all along, waiting for a chance to git rid of us for good. We used the mule and horses as shields. He killed them. I guess he thought we'd drowned. If it hadn't been for Pedro, we would have. Driftwood was floating by. We hung onto a big tree, hiding among the branches and drifted downstream. It was almost dark when we got ashore. How we lived through the night I'll never know. We knew Zack would show up here sooner or later, if he was still alive. After all, the Sioux might have got him. I guess the thought of coming into ownership of the *Si-Si* kept him going in spite of everything. It seems to have become an obsession with him. Think of all the years he had it in mind, all the scheming and planning."

Her father came from the room into which Zack had been carried. "I think Pedro's right," he said. "Zack ought to pull through. He'll live, at least until he can stand trial and be hanged."

He looked at Val and wagged his shaggy head. "No," he admitted, "I might have strung you up with my own hands, but I was spared that. I'm no longer trying to put myself ahead of the law nor condemn any human being without a trial. Even Zack. Vengeance is mine, says the law. That's the way it will be from now on."

He added, "Pride goeth before a fall. Even Sheila never knew Zack was my sister's adopted son. Zack made sort of a deal with me. Neither of us was to mention it. I was ashamed of my own sister. I was so hidebound I never wanted even my sons an' daughter to know about her, but I guess they knew. They didn't know Zack was the son of the man who had led her astray. I let Zack sort of blackmail me into treatin' him better'n he deserved. I admit he earned his way. He was a good range boss. Why, I even intended to remember him in my will. I told him so. Not a fortune, of course, but enough to stake him for years. Maybe that's what got him covetin' all of it."

"Speaking of wills," Val said. "I don't believe you know that Zack made out one in Wagonbow, naming you and Sheila as his heirs."

"He did?" Cass exclaimed.

"Of course his real idea was to establish some sort of legal proof that he was your affectionate heir, and also your only heir, so as to help him when he laid claim to *Si-Si*."

Cass rubbed his chin thoughtfully. "He

figgered out everything, didn't he? So I'm *his* heir, am I? Maybe that takes care of a little matter that's been troublin' me. A matter of about $10,000 in gold."

"What do you mean?" Sheila asked.

"It seems to me that Zack is the one who finally brought Val to me, ain't he? Therefore it also seems to me that I can decide he's the one entitled to the reward."

"Zack?" Sheila exclaimed incredulously. "You mean to give him all that money? Are you out of your mind?"

"It won't take long to extradite him to New Mexico," her father said. "I'll see to that. Chances are he'll swing. Me an' Sheila are his only heirs, ain't we?"

It took a moment or two for that to sink in. "Why — why, you old schemer!" Sheila said helplessly.

"Hola!" Pedro exclaimed. "I salute you, *el patrón!* You are one very, very smart man."

"Hold on!" Val said, grinning. "Zack, whether he hangs or gets a life term, could change his will."

"We'd still be his heirs," Cass grunted. "Any court would uphold us. Any court in New Mexico, that is. I have many friends there. Especially so when they know my share is going to you."

"To me?" Val echoed.

258

"I'll draw up an assignment as soon as I can get a lawyer out to the ranch. I'm turning over any such money to you." Cass added wryly, "It's only a little down payment on what I owe you."

"I'll hold onto the other half for a while," Sheila spoke. "At least until I see what he does with your half. So much money might go to his head."

Val's grin widened. "There's a person named Henry Erskine who'll be pulling into Fort Steele in a day or two who will be mighty disappointed when he hears about this. He thinks the money should go to him, or those near him. He'll probably sue."

"Let him," Cass said. "Sheila told me about the Erskines. The money's on deposit in a bank in Santa Fe. That is in New Mexico also. In New Mexico I pay rewards to who I danged well want to. Now, getting back to what we were talkin' about, I don't savvy why Zack took so long after Boone was in his grave to go after the rest o' the family."

"For one thing he may have decided to lay low for a few years after Boone was killed," Sheila said. "He probably lost his nerve for a while. More likely, it was lack of opportunity. Remember, Dad, that you sent me away to school at Santa Fe right after

Boone's death. And then to New Orleans for nearly four winters. I was gone the biggest part of the time, coming back to the ranch just for short vacations. Penny, being only a child, was watched over by the nurses and wives of the *vaqueros*."

"And for another thing . . . ?" Val urged, still grinning.

She wrinkled her nose disapprovingly at him. "I was eighteen by the time I'd finished school and came back to the ranch," she said. "Zack — well he — well he —"

"What she means," Val said, "is that Zack noticed that she was turning out to be not so bad-looking after all. Fact is, she still might be halfway pretty after she's fattened up a little."

"There are others around here who also need some tallow on them, not to mention a bath or two," she said. "Have you looked at yourself in a mirror, my friend?"

"Not lately," Val said. "We were talking about how Zack decided he'd try a better and safer way of getting his hands on the C-Bar-C. Marry into it."

"The whelp!" Cass roared. "So that was it?"

"I discouraged him, of course," Sheila said. "In fact, I had to almost use a quirt on him once. He told me I'd change my mind and that he'd wait. He didn't really give up until you decided to sell out in New Mexico and move to northern range. After that I really became afraid of him. I suppose that was when he went back to his original plan of getting rid of me and Penny, and then you."

"I never knew he was botherin' you," her father said. "You should have told me."

Val lifted Penny in his arms and kissed her. "Ever been kissed by a scarecrow before, Penny?" he asked.

"I wish you'd shave, Mr. Man," Penny said.

"As soon as possible," Val promised. "And, at first chance, I'm buying you the prettiest doll I can find. The other one is in an army ambulance with an outfit that should be pulling into town any day. That one we will keep forever. A treasure. I hope you're not too grown-up to play with dolls."

"You know I love dollies, Mr. Man," Penny said.

He looked at Sheila. "I know how you stand about dolls," he said. "But what about unwashed scarecrows?"

Her eyes began to dance. "That depends."

"On what?"

"Well, on many things. Some I've traveled with have had their good points. Isn't that so, Pedro?"

Pedro eyed Val pityingly. "It seems, *amigo,* that you have not escaped after all. You have been captured."

"Having been acquainted with a number of would-be lady-killers down in New Mexico," Val said to Sheila, "I take it that Zack was not the only one who discovered that you weren't exactly homely."

"There were several," she said. "In fact, quite a number."

"Did you have to use a quirt on any of them also?"

"That seems to me to be a matter that does not concern you, my scarecrow friend."

"Indeed it does," Val said. "Better reach for your quirt."

He took her in his arms and kissed her resoundingly. Sheila did not resist. After a time she murmured softly, "I've waited quite a few years for this. I've had this scarecrow singled out for me ever since I first began worrying about freckles on my nose. But you were right, Penny. He does need a shave."

Cass spoke to Pedro as they left the room, arm-in-arm. "At least I have one son after all."

"And soon more grandchildren," Pedro predicted.

The employees of Thorndike Press hope you have enjoyed this Large Print book. All our Large Print titles are designed for easy reading, and all our books are made to last. Other Thorndike Press Large Print books are available at your library, through selected bookstores, or directly from us.

For information about titles, please call:

(800) 223-1244
(800) 223-6121

To share your comments, please write:

Publisher
Thorndike Press
P.O. Box 159
Thorndike, Maine 04986